A Whiskey Sour Wipeout

by

Constance Barker

Sign up for Constance Barker's <u>New Releases Newsletter</u>
I will never spam or sell your email address

Chapter One

"Git out of there you old coot!" Dixie scolded Digger for sneaking an olive from the condiment tray.

"What? I didn't eat lunch today. Give me a break." Digger flashed her his version of a smile, but it looked more like he had indigestion.

"If you eat anymore I'm going to have to charge you for it. If you're that hungry, order a plate. You know we sell food here, too, not just beer." Dixie glared out the side of her face at the grave digger.

"I'm good. Thanks." Digger scanned the two empty seats next to him. "Where's Guardrail and Dog Breath? I haven't seen much of them lately."

Dixie wiped the bar surface and didn't look up. "They are busy with some big customization job. I heard Dog mention dual sidecars, or something like that. They've been busy at work."

Digger swiveled his head round to scan the bar and dining area. "This place feels empty. Guardrail and Dog are working. Ginger, Ida and Piper are out playing journalist. Half our crew is missing today."

Dixie flicked her wrist and checked the watch strapped there. "Ginger said they will be back, in a couple of hours. Piper's syndicated articles are generating a lot of attention and the girls are working on another one for next month. Seems everyone wants to know more about our little pub. It's good for business."

A voice emanated through the order window. "Hey, you know I'm here, right? I can hear you back here. Why does everyone always forget about me?" Bones was busy washing dishes as indicated by the sounds of clinking plates and sloshing water.

"We know you're there, Bones. Now get back to work!" Tom was talking to Star over by the souvenir racks till he spun to yell at Bones. Then he turned to face his gloomy patron. "And what are you talking about, Digger? What are we chopped liver? There are plenty of people here."

Star smiled at Digger, and he blushed. She said, "I know you miss your drinking buddies. I was hoping to chat with Dog myself."

"Whenever you say 'I know' it makes my skin crawl. Makes me feel like you're in my head, reading my thoughts. Ya know, the psychic thing." Digger couldn't look at her and stared down at the foam on his beer.

She chuckled at him. "No! It's not like that at all. It's not hard for anyone to see that you miss Guardrail and Dog when they're not here."

Tom grunted. "I miss them too. Guardrail and Dog are some of my best paying customers. Now where were we, ah yes, the T-shirts."

Star picked one up and examined it. "I like them. It gets the grumpy chicken right, too."

Tom scowled. "The image is kind of creepy. You think people will buy them?"

Star chuckled. "Yeah. This is what people have been asking for. To see what she looks like."

The front door popped open and in walked the big frame of Guardrail with Dog Breath in tow. The two marched over to their stools like they owned the room and assumed their spots next to Digger. Guardrail boomed. "Dixie, you pretty thing. Two tall cold ones. We're celebrating the completion of a huge job."

Digger looked up from his beer and beamed. "Glad to see you boys."

Dog Breath, for once in his life, wore a smile on his face. Dixie noticed and asked, "What canary did you swallow? I almost didn't recognize you with that silly grin."

"Taught Guardrail something on this job. We would never have finished the job if I didn't know how do it." Dog nodded to emphasize his bragging rights.

Guardrail responded by punching him in the shoulder and Dog almost fell off the stool. "Don't get a big head. It was not that big a deal."

Dog rubbed his shoulder and reset himself properly on the stool. "That's the thanks I get. And you wonder why I don't smile much."

Tom snarled at the two motorcycle mechanics. "We don't give a hoot about your chopping and welding escapades. What do you think of these T-shirts?" Tom held one up so they could see it.

Dog answered him, "Is kind of creepy. But I like it. It's a good likeness of the cranky bird."

Guardrail added, "Printed on the black T-shirts like that, it looks like a T-shirt from an old heavy metal band. Looks good."

Star grinned. "See, people will buy them."

Tom snorted, and put the T-shirt down. Between the sales in the pub and at Star's new age store, the merchandise business was a good money maker. And Tom liked making the extra money, so he paid more attention than needed to the souvenirs.

"I am glad you came in while I was here. Can I talk to you, in private Dog?" Star's voice was soft and had a hint of nerves.

"Me? What do you need to talk to me about?" Dog's eyebrows hiked up about an inch as he replied.

"It's a little private, we can talk over there." Star pointed at an empty table in one corner of the dining area.

"Okay." Dog slowly rose, then hesitated for a moment before following Star to the corner table.

Star had a fifteen-foot lead and got to the table first, taking a seat and folding her hands on the tabletop. Then she waited for Dog.

Dog was a few seconds behind her and stood behind a tucked in chair. "Okay, this is weird. So, what did you want to talk about."

"Take a seat. I would like to get a read on you. Something strange happened and I fear something bad is happening in your life." Star pointed to the empty chair in front of him.

Dog took the offer, slid the chair out from under the table and sat, placing the beer he brought on the flat surface. "I'm not trying to hurt your feelings, but that is the kind of talk that makes everyone think you are a little, well, odd and scary at times."

Star laughed. "I have been psychic since I was a young girl. And I know that my gifts and visions can spook people."

Dog leaned in to her, just a little bit, and used his best compassionate voice, "Do you really think the abilities you have are gifts?"

She giggled. "Of course. The ability to communicate with those who have passed to the other side is wonderful. And people have always wanted to see the future. When my visions and dreams indicate a possible future, that is special. Not everyone can do those things. So, yes, it can be scary sometimes but it is without a doubt a gift."

Dog shuddered. "I don't get it, I guess."

"Dog, listen, I had a dream. A man was murdered by a

woman, using some sort of poison."

Dog huffed. "I don't see what that has to do with me."

Star shifted in her seat. "I was not done. The man talked about his old 'Nam friends and your name was mentioned a few times. The name Dog Breath is not very common, so it had to be you."

Dog's face went long. "Did you get the man's name?"

"I think the woman called him Harry once." Star scrunched up her face and looked off into space. "That's all I could make out. Does the name Harry mean anything to you?"

Dog froze, then stammered. "That is so general. I knew many Harrys in my life. And your dreams don't always mean what you think. You told me that yourself."

"That's true. But I know when to pay attention. And we need to pay attention to this." Star pleaded with her eyes for him to understand.

Dog could be a bit oblivious at times, but he understood her message. "Okay. I get it. But right now, my life is really good. And there are no Harrys in my life."

Star smiled and spoke in a low but serious tone. "Just keep your guard up. Something is going on. I know it."

Dog frowned. "See, there it is again. That weird poltergeist stuff. And I hate when your voice gets that weird tone! I think we are done and I am going to go back and drink some beer, celebrate with my buddies. You want to come join us or do you have more to say?"

"I told you what I can for now. If I learn anything else, I will tell you, promise. Can you do the same? If something strange does happen, you need to tell me. Alright?"

Dog smiled. "You will be the first to know. I promise."

Dixie shrieked, followed by the sound of a glass breaking on the floor. "Jumping chicken livers!"

Digger leaned over the bar. "Are you all right, Dixie? What happened?"

Dixie's voice was raised a few octaves. "Can't you tell I'm not alright?"

Guardrail boomed, "No, what happened?"

Dixie picked up a pub glass and pulled the tap. Thick black beer flowed. "This is the lager tap, not the stout tap. It should be light gold and clear. But it looks like molasses and stinks. The grumper is up to something, that is the only possible explanation. I just poured a dozen beers from this tap and it was fine until now."

Guardrail glanced briefly at the pickled egg jar. "You sure it's that pesky limping chicken spirit? The eggs are her favorite thing to mess with. And they're fine."

Digger added, "Guardrail is right. Just change the keg. Maybe it needs to be changed."

Tom jumped in. "I'll change it. No one messes with my taps."

Tom grabbed Bones and the two carried out a brand-new keg from the walk-in cooler. Then they unhooked the tap from the problem keg and removed it.

Bones shook his head. "I don't know. This still feels like it has beer."

Tom barked back at him. "Be quiet and help me put this new keg in the chill box."

The two wrestled the heavy keg into place, then Tom tapped it. He pulled the tap and clear, golden lager flowed. "See, everything is fine."

Guardrail exhaled. "Whew! That's good. I think my blood pressure skyrocketed when it looked like we were having problem with pouring beer. And just when I got here."

Dixie grabbed a pint glass and poured. "Here ya go big fella. Nothing to worry about." She put the fresh drink down in front of Guardrail.

Guardrails eyes enlarged and sparkled. "That's beautiful. The perfect pour. I could float a quarter on that head of foam. Just lovely."

Star and Dog Breath had moved from their private spot back over to the bar with all the commotion and Dog sat on his usual stool.

Star took a stool near the center of the bar. She leaned

on the edge and asked, "You okay Dixie? There's glass everywhere back there. Did you get cut?"

Dixie shook her head no. "I'm fine. But that was really strange."

Bones came out with a broom and dust pan and helped Dixie clean up the mess. Bones gasped, "Man! This stuff stinks. I'm not drinking anything that smells like this. I can't believe it came from a keg."

Dixie glared at the young man. "It was fine until I pulled that last glass."

Tom came behind the bar with a big smile on his face. "Think I will have to do some quality control on that newly tapped keg." He grabbed a pilsner glass and pulled the tap. After a couple of seconds, Tom whimpered and dropped the glass, which shattered on the floor.

The group at the bar stared at the broken glass on the floor, then stared at Tom.

Star finally asked, "Did you get cut? And what is that weird black stuff on the floor."

Tom whimpered. "I'm alright. That stuff came out of the tap." He pointed at the puddle on the floor.

Dog moaned and looked to Star. "Something *is* going on. Nothing like this has happened in the pub for months. And this happens just after you have a dream? Even I know this isn't a coincidence."

Star raised one eyebrow a little. "I told you I know what dreams to pay attention to and this recent one was definitely one of them. I agree this is no coincidence. The grumpy chicken is sending us a warning."

Chapter Two

Things had been quiet for months...I even worried that the grumpy chicken had left our pub and gone somewhere else. But that all changed yesterday when our taps acted up for no apparent reason. Well, Star did have a dream and I've learned from experience to pay attention when she tells us about something strange.

"I didn't sleep a wink last night. Why do things like this happen to me?" Dog Breath's eyes were a bit droopy and he yawned.

Tom snorted, "I was the one who poured that foul glass of, whatever that was, yesterday."

"Yeah, and we've had to listen to ya bellyaching ever since. It wasn't that big a deal and the beer has flowed fine since." Guardrail rolled his eyes and took a bite from the sandwich he ordered for lunch.

Ida shrugged her shoulders. "Guardrail's right. It's not that big a deal. And we were searching for things to include in Piper's next newspaper article, so this actually is a good thing from that perspective. Now we have something to write about."

Dog shook his head slowly. "Not a good thing. Not good at all. Something bizarre is going on. I know it."

Digger had been still and quiet but laughed. "You are the most pessimistic person I know. Your business is doing good and you have caring friends to rely on. What's there to worry about?"

Everyone stared at Digger.

Ida glared at the old grave digger and spoke. "Really? You're calling someone out about being pessimistic? That's a bit ironic, in my humble opinion."

"I'm a happy, optimistic man." Digger scanned his friend's faces, then added, "Sometimes."

The snicker slipped out of me. "I'm sorry, Digger, but Ida is right. You can be a little gloomy and gruff sometimes."

Digger shrugged the comments off. "Ginger, I don't care what y'all think." Then he swigged his beer to ignore us.

Piper discounted the conversation up until now and decided to change the topic. "So, where is Star? I need to talk to her to make sure we accurately recount what she told Dog in the article. You know, exactly what she saw in her dream."

I answered her. "She said she was coming by later tonight."

"Ginger, do you like these T-shirts?" Tom was over by the souvenir rack and held up one of the new designs.

I chuckled. "Looks like it came from a heavy metal concert Dad."

Guardrail slapped the bar top. "I said the same thing when I saw it."

Piper sighed. "Come on guys. The T-shirts can wait. I have a deadline to make and I need your help with the new article."

Dog sat up straight and pinched his eyebrows. "The events from yesterday aren't enough for you? You're getting lazy and been spoiled by our spirit chicken. You got plenty for a new article."

Piper frowned. "I know there is enough for an article. But I have a better chance of getting the story straight by talking to these walls. Not one of you knows how to focus and relay details."

Tom huffed. "I can. I will tell you all you need to know. Star told Dog about a bonkers dream and our taps spit out weird, dark colored beer. Then it stopped. The end."

Piper grunted. "See what I have to deal with?" She then locked eyes with Tom for twenty seconds until he lost the staring contest when he waved his hand at her.

Tom bellowed, "Quit your belly aching. You'll get what ya need from Star."

Dixie squealed and we all spun to the sound. "Sorry, the beer I was pouring made a gurgling sound. I thought maybe it was happening again." Dixie let out a nervous laugh and held up the beer for all to see.

Tom walked behind the bar and pushed Dixie aside. "Let me see."

Guardrail leaned on the bar and his voice became firm and loud. "I told you before. Don't tell me the beer is messed up. We got no other place to go and drink with friends."

Piper chuckled. "Oh, what was that? The tap hiccups and that becomes a crisis."

A strange low grinding of metal on metal drifted out of the kitchen through the order window. It made an eerie sound that made your skin crawl. I saw Dixie's face go white and my dad froze in his steps. He hollered, "Bones, what was that?"

"Sorry, dragged the grease pan out from under the

grill. It somehow got stuck and I had to give it a little persuasion." Bones' hand popped through the order window, and he gave the thumbs up to confirm it was alright.

"You break that grill I am going to break you. And it's coming out of your pay!" Dad hated the thought of not being able to sell beer or food.

Piper mumbled, commiserating with herself. "Now it's the grill."

"Hey, Ginger, do you know anyone named Harry?" Dog was back to worrying about Star's dream.

"Yeah, Harry Connick, Jr." I smiled at Dog but he looked back at me like I spoke to him in Latin.

Dog scrunched his face. "Who's that?"

Ida snarked, "Really, you don't know who that is?"

Dog raised his eyebrows. "Am I supposed to?"

Ida chuckled. "No, I guess not."

Piper slapped her forehead. "I think this conversation is shrinking my brain."

Tom asked, "Who is Harry Connick? And why should we care?"

I threw my head back. "Dad, forget it. I was just trying to have a little fun with Dog."

Dog hung his head and talked to the beer in front of

him. "Why couldn't Star see just a little more in that dream."

Bones yelled from the back. "What about Harry Houdini?"

Tom spun and glared at the order window. He considered yelling at the young grill cook, but decided to play along. "And what about Harry Belafonte."

Ida added, "And Harry Chapin."

Digger tried. "Harry Manilow." Oh Lordy!

The chatter fell quiet and I was not sure where or who to look at.

Piper corrected. "Digger, I believe you meant Barry Manilow. But thanks for playing."

The giggles made Digger turn red. "I should just keep my mouth shut. I make it too easy for y'all to make fun of me."

I consoled him. "We're not making fun of you. Just having a little fun."

Digger grunted. "Yeah, at my expense."

"Hey Digger, I love the deep voice of that singer Harry White!" Ida barely got the sentence out with all the tittering.

The chuckling became infectious and soon the pub was a roar of laughter. It was so loud Dog Breath almost didn't hear the sound. His phone was ringing.

Dog pulled the noisy thing from his pocket and answered. "Guard Dog Custom Motorcycles... Yeah, this is Jimmy Bell... What? Lugnut? How did it happen?... Heart attack, that's awful... Thanks for calling." Then he clicked off.

After putting the phone back in his pocket. He glanced around and I could see he was white. Everyone else must have seen, too, because the pub became quiet. I asked, "Dog, what was that all about?"

"My best friend from the motor pool in 'Nam died. We called him Lugnut. He and I did everything together over there. He even gave me the name Dog Breath." Dog's voice was soft and choppy. He dropped his chin a little.

"I'm so sorry, buddy." Guardrail put his arm around his business partner.

"We all are. Is there anything we can do?" Dixie moved over to him and gently caressed his hand on the bar.

Dog raised his chin up. "That's not the worst of it. I never even put two and two together. Lugnut's real name was Harry Campbell."

Dixie took two steps back. "Star's dream is coming true."

Chapter Three

"What am I doing?!" Slick scolded himself as he hoisted himself up and over the living room window sill. He knew this window would be unlocked, but it was six feet up off the ground. The inverted five-gallon pail he found served as a step, but it still took some work to pull his old body up into the window opening. He should have brought a ladder or step stool.

Breaking and entering was a new adventure for him. Slick pushed paper for a living in an office. He had always been a desk jockey, even when serving as a clerk in the motor pool in Vietnam.

"What the…" Slick tripped on a pile of old Playboys and laughed out loud. Lugnut always liked the ladies, but this was an odd spot for a pile of magazines. Then Slick realized this was just one of three piles. Guess Lugnut had been collecting them for a while. "I can't believe Bianca agreed to this." Slick was not sure why he was talking to himself, but he guessed it might be his way of coping with the nerves.

Slick took out the flashlight he brought and clicked it on. Nothing. He banged the base of the dark torch with his free hand. Nothing. "Only I can take a flashlight to a break in that has dead batteries."

Unscrewing the base of the stubborn flashlight, he took out the D batteries and one was leaking. Before he could cuss, he saw a flashlight on Lugnut's coffee table. Sometimes luck is on your side. He grabbed the tactical flashlight off the coffee table and threw the switch. A beam of light burst forth. Slick was back in business.

Then he moved into the bedroom cautiously. Slick knew the place should be empty. Bianca, Lugnut's wife, had gone to stay with her sister after the heart attack. She took Lugnut's death hard, and didn't want to be in a house full of reminders.

He had no plausible reason to be in Lugnut's house, so it was best to keep a low profile to keep a nosy neighbor or someone else from noticing his presence. He kept telling himself better safe than sorry.

On entering the master bedroom, he saw the bed was made and the window was cracked to let in fresh air. "Ah, come on. I could have just come in this window instead. It's so much closer to the ground."

After lodging the complaint with himself, he began his search. He wasn't sure, but Lugnut's heart attack didn't sit right with him. Something else was going on, he was sure of it. And he was here to get the proof.

He checked the dresser and was surprised how clean and neat it was. This was clearly one of Bianca's claimed spots and he admired the pretty jewelry box perched on a doily in the center of the dresser top. He didn't know why, it must have been simple curiosity, but he opened it. It was mostly empty and he wasn't surprised. Neither he nor Lugnut ever made much money, but they got by. He closed the lid, leaving the contents undisturbed.

Next, he checked the night stands but came up empty. Slick stood straight and rubbed his forehead with his eyes closed. "Think, you dummy. Where would Lugnut keep them?"

Slick's eyes popped open and he headed straight for the small half bath off the bedroom. It was an example of organized chaos. Toiletries, toothbrushes, and vitamin bottles occupied every flat surface. He had some work to do, so he began looking. He started with bottles of vitamins and looked at each bottle, one by one, till he spotted a small bottle and picked it up. He shone the beam from his hand-held tactile light onto it and read the label. "That's the one." He then put the bottle in his pocket and headed for the kitchen.

Once in the kitchen he stood in the center and collected his thoughts. "If he thinks like me, and I know he does, he would have it tacked to the fridge with a magnet." Slick found the fridge and scanned the numerous pieces of paper held there by dozens of magnets. At one particular note, he stopped and read it slowly. "Bingo!"

Slick took the note and put it in his pocket along with the small bottle. Then he ran his eyes over the place one more time. What was he forgetting? While he was here, might as well get all that he could.

Then the kitchen lit up with headlights from a car. He

crouched down to hide and peeked out the window, covertly. He saw a car pulling into Lugnut's driveway. This was not good.

Slick made a beeline for the broom closet. He quietly climbed in and turned off the flashlight. Then he closed the door, leaving it cracked a half inch so he could see whoever came into the house.

As he leaned to peek out from his hiding spot, the ironing board fell over smacking him in the back. Slick almost fainted. This was not in the plan and he hated being trapped, but what other choice was there.

***

Linzi Howard put the key in the lock and opened the door. She should not be doing this, but she had to retrieve the bottle. Besides, she had previously offered to help the family make the funeral arrangements and they had given her the key to the place to keep an eye on it. So, if anyone did see her, she had an excuse to be here.

She tried to keep quiet and avoided turning on the lights. It served no purpose to call more attention to her presence than necessary. But the stealthy plan proved to be a mistake when she banged her knee on the coffee table. Linzi cussed under her breath and hopped on one leg around the living room, while grabbing her aching knee.

"Son of a… I told him a hundred times to move that stinking thing. And who needs a coffee table that big!"

Linzi squinted in the dark to see that she had knocked a number of empty beer bottles over onto the floor. "I don't know what I saw in him. What a slob. He never picked up after himself." She scanned the scene one more time. "Come to think of it, what was he doing drinking this much beer. He never listened to anyone. I can't believe his sorry excuse for a wife would let him do that!" She shook her head at all the beer bottles.

Linzi then sat on the couch and turned on one of the table lamps in the living room to examine her knee. She was bleeding but she would live. However, she now walked more slowly, and with a slight limp. Despite the injury, she went back to it and kept on moving. She had a job to do and the sooner it was completed, the better.

***

Slick watched her from his hiding spot in the nearby broom closet. Linzi wore her scrubs and still had her name tag pinned on her chest. She clearly was coming home from work. Was she looking for the same thing he was?

Linzi headed for the master bedroom and Slick lost sight of her. But he did hear her cussing and sounds that indicated she was throwing things on the floor in the master bathroom. Apparently, she could not find what she came for.

Then she stormed back into the living room. She tossed everything on the coffee and end tables, frantically looking for something. But, she didn't appear to find it.

She stood up straight and shouted at the ceiling. "Where did you put it, you good for nothing liar."

Slick put his hand over his mouth to stop from laughing. He was now certain he beat her to the goods by just a few minutes. Maybe he was not a professional break-in artist, but he sure beat her to the punch on this one.

Linzi went into the bedroom again, and from the sounds Slick heard, he guessed she was ransacking the half bath. After five minutes, she emerged once again in the living room. And it was not good. She was smiling and fussed with her hair. She always pushed the loose locks from her face using the back of her hand when she was being smug, just like she was doing now. She must have found what she was looking for.

Slick could feel his heart rate speed up and he tried to stop the heavy breathing. He was sure she might hear him wheezing with anxiety in the closet. But, Linzi didn't take long to turn off the table light she turned on earlier, and left in a hurry. She hadn't even bothered to pick up the bottles or any of the items she'd knocked over or tossed on the floor during her search.

Now Slick was alone again. And he needed to think. What did she find? What did he miss? Slick still had some work to do and went back to search Lugnut's place one more time. This was going to be harder than he thought and maybe he should get someone to help. He was coming to realize that he was well out of his element.

Chapter Four

Star flipped the sign on the front door to display "closed," then locked the main entrance. She was glad this day was coming to an end. Nothing went right and she could not escape the feeling that something was off.

While performing a reading for a customer, she stumbled to see things clearly. For the first time, Star's abilities alluded her and the confidence she normally had was lacking in her session with a good client.

Then the coffeemaker broke. Star saved for a while to get one of the fancy pod devices. She always wanted to have a fresh, quality cup of coffee at anytime with just the push of a button. But the pump on her new unit gave out before it was even a month old. She hoped it was still under warranty.

On top of the broken appliance, the pen she forgot about in her purse leaked, and ink on her fingers somehow managed to get on her favorite dress. Now it had two big, blue spots she knew would not come out.

And if that wasn't enough, the toilet started to run uncontrollably. Star called a plumber since it took her a few minutes to figure out how to simply turn off the water to the toilet. And now she was forced to turn the water supply on, and then off, every time she used the bathroom. She already missed the convenience of just flushing.

But the work day was over and Star needed to tidy things up a bit. She started by putting away the Tarot cards. Then she moved on to cleaning the plastic cups and napkins off the big table that occupied the center of her new age shop. After everything was in its place, she grabbed her ink filled purse and headed for the back door.

She exited as usual, locked the back door and headed for her car. Everyone has a bad day every now and then, and this was one of hers. It was a doozy, but now, it was over.

On entering her small apartment, the black cat named Morgan le Fay meowed profusely while circling a dish on the floor. Star immediately noticed the empty food bowl, so she opened a fresh can of food and fed it to Morgan.

She grimaced while removing the ink blot dress and put it on top of the hamper to bring to the dry cleaners. It was worth asking the pros if they thought it was salvageable, but she already knew the answer.

Then she threw on her robe. She was ready for a long, hot shower. But her hunger overruled, so a quick snack was in order before washing.

The only thing she had that was quick was some toaster tarts. So, she threw in a couple of hot fudge sundae. Chocolate, the day was looking up.

She plunked down on the couch to wait for her toaster pastries to cook. While she waited, she opened the mail. Turned out she must've forgotten to pay the water bill last month and now she was overdue. She scowled at the piece of paper like it was lying, then flung it on the coffee table. Seems the bad day was not over yet.

Then the toaster caught on fire. The flames shot out like a fire cracker. Star grabbed the spray nozzle from the sink and put the flames out. Now, she had a smoke-filled apartment with a water-soaked kitchen floor. That is when the smoke alarm went off. Seems her chocolate treat was not meant to be.

The incident was the last straw and Star felt the tears well up in her eyes. But she gritted her teeth, opened a window, and fanned the white, round puck shaped smoke alarm till the fresh air caused it to fall silent.

She knew that she needed something to settle her rattled set of nerves and decided, just like her water bill, the shower was overdue. So, she headed for the bathroom.

Star started her routine and went to grab a clean towel. Turns out, she had none and she actually chuckled a little at the predicament. It was not that big a deal and it just meant it was time to do laundry. Besides, she could just find the least dirty towel, fluff it up, and roll it up to make it seem like a clean towel from a high-class spa.

Part of her knew she was making excuses, trying to justify cutting corners to get through her horrible day. But what else was there to do, sometimes you just have to do what you must and move on.

Morgan found her while she was folding the dirty towel and rubbed on her legs. It was funny how the feeling of a cat grazing her calves could be so soothing to her, and annoying, all at the same time.

Star put the neatly rolled towel on the corner of the vanity and reached down to pet the kitty. But she didn't raise her head and purr, instead the cat sprinted off to the kitchen. It was odd, so she gave chase to see what was so urgent for her feline friend.

Once in the kitchen, she saw Morgan check her water bowl. It was empty and she must have missed it when she filled the food bowl. Star felt guilty and poured a saucer of milk and put it down for her pet. She asked herself out loud, "How could I miss her empty water bowl?"

Star was now certain. Something was trying to get her attention, but she had no idea what it was. But she could no longer deny it, she was distracted. This was something she never experienced before and she struggled to put the pieces together.

After taking a deep breath, she forced herself to gain control of the situation and it was finally time to shower. Just the thought of the warm water washing over her made her feel a little better. She headed once again for the bathroom.

She nudged the shower curtain aside just enough to reach in and feel for the water knobs. She turned on the water, then waited for the hot water to arrive. She loved her apartment, but the hot water took too long to get to the shower. In the meantime, she may as well get things ready and she laid out the toiletries she would need after washing.

Morgan showed up while she made sure there was toothpaste. After all the things that went wrong today, double checking everything seemed like a good idea. And the cat must have wanted to help, because it jumped up on the vanity to see what she was doing.

Star was too frazzled from the day's events that it was no use shooing Morgan away. She just left her there next to the sink, then lost the robe and zipped open the shower curtain.

It was impossible to tell which was louder, her screams or the cat's snarling and hissing. Both were reacting to the apparition in front of them. The ghost was a man floating in the middle of her shower. He was holding his chest from what Star could tell. But it was hard because a strange, bright light blared from her shower and almost obscured the floating apparition.

With one last burst of light, Star thought she heard a few words followed by nothing. It all disappeared. The words rattled in her brain for a minute, then it felt like she recognized them. The spirit may have said, "Help Dog Breath."

Through shear will, Star closed her eyes and forced herself to settle down. When she reopened her eyelids, the first thing she realized was Morgan had exited the tiny bathroom and she was alone. Star guessed the cat was hiding under the bed. And that is when she grasped she was standing there naked, shivering.

Star grabbed her robe and threw it back on. Then she headed into the bedroom. Star needed to get dressed and find Dog Breath, now. Things were happening in the spirit world and Dog was at the center of it all. And he was in danger. It was the only way to explain this spirit becoming so bold.

Chapter Five

Digger and Guardrail tried their best to console Dog Breath. But it was futile. The sight of his friends offering support warmed my heart, and my concern for him dominated my thoughts.

I instinctively used my soft, understanding voice, "Dog, we are all sorry that you lost your friend. Is there anything we can do?

"Yeah, come on buddy. Listen to Ginger. What can we do to help? Did this old 'Nam friend of yours have family? Maybe they need some help. You should stop feeling bad for yourself and see if they are alright."

Piper stared at the big man and blinked a few times as she searched for her words. "That was compassionate to worry about the man's family, Guardrail. But, at the same time, aren't you being a little hard on Dog? They served together in Vietnam and he has suffered a great loss."

Digger sat next to Dog and patted him on the back. Digger also nodded no. "Dog is feeling the loss, sure, but I don't think you understand. He is worried about Star's dream. And don't forget the taps acting up. We all know what happens when the Grumper starts acting up like that. The taps were no fluke...it was our ghost chicken trying to warn us."

The front door opened and the two spinster sisters entered. Edith announced their presence. "Hello everybody! We missed you all so much. And what did we miss? Lily has been under the weather the last couple of days, but she is feeling better and we thought we would come by to see what's going on?"

Piper chuckled. "Well, go on Tom. Give 'em one of your one-of-a-kind summaries."

Tom shrugged. "Star had a weird dream and our taps belched some weird, black, smelly beer. Then Dog's old war buddy had a heart attack and died. See, Piper, it's not that hard."

Lily and Edith pinched their eyebrows like they were just tasked with cracking the mystery of life. Lily spoke, "Well, that was concise, but not entirely helpful."

I smiled at Lily's honesty. "We missed you both. Have a seat, ladies, and we'll fill you in on some of the details."

As Lily and Edith grabbed a seat at their usual table, the front door flew open once again and banged loudly on the bump stop. In the door frame stood Star, her blouse half tucked and her hair a mess. She always looked so pretty and composed, I almost didn't recognize her like this and asked, "What happened to you? You look a little… well, off."

Star took a few steps into the pub and shut the door. "That's an understatement, Ginger. A spirit has been stalking me all day until it finally appeared in front of me. But it chose an odd place and time. As I threw open the curtain to take a shower, it was hovering in my tub."

Digger shook his head like the information he just learned hurt. "Wait, a spirit stalked you? How can it do that? And it saw you naked in the shower?

Star blushed. "Thanks Digger. Now everyone is imagining me naked in the shower."

Guardrail shrugged. "Not m…Ah, who am I kidding?"

I tried to help Star and change the subject. "That sounds horrible. It's almost like that scene from the movie Psycho."

Piper added, "Well not just like that scene, Ginger. The ghost was in the shower and you were looking in. Right?" Piper stared at Star for confirmation.

Star nodded yes.

Edith spoke up. "That's not important. Can't you see the poor girl is shaken?"

Dog had been quiet for a while, but broke his temporary silence. "I'm not surprised that something happened to you, Star. But, I am sorry about it for you, that it shook you up. By the way, you should know. I figured out who Harry is and he died this afternoon."

Star rushed over to Dog and grabbed his arm. "What? What are you talking about? Who was Harry? Tell me." She was almost frantic. Now, I understood why she looked unkempt.

"He was my best friend in Vietnam. We went through a lot together. But no one ever called him Harry. Heck, most didn't even know his real name. We all knew him as Lugnut."

Star's eyes drooped on hearing of Dog's loss. "I'm so sorry, Dog. I know your Army friends are important to you. Are you okay?"

Dog studied the disheveled Star for a second. "I could ask you the same thing."

Star blushed and chuckled at the same time, then said, "I'm fine. I rushed over after the spirit appeared, to make sure you were alright. But I am actually a little relieved now because I think this is all starting to make some sense. But I'm not sure my cat is ever coming out from under the bed."

"Well, if it makes sense to you, maybe you can share. I am beyond confused." Dog tried to smile but his sadness prevented it from happening.

Star took a deep breath. "You must have been important to Harry…"

Dog cut her off. "It's Lugnut, no one calls him Harry. Remember?"

Dixie scrunched her face. "What is it with you military men and nicknames. Dog Breath? Lugnut? Those aren't even real names. And who comes up with them?"

Dog shrugged. "It's just the way it is."

Star sighed. "Alright, *Lugnut* must have been a good friend. I think it was his spirit in my shower and he was worried about you. I am sure of it. And now that I'm in The Grumpy Chicken, I'm getting a feeling. The chicken is relieved that we are starting to figure things out. She is trying to help us." Star scanned the dining room as if she was trying to see the chicken or another spirit in the dining room.

Dog held up two fingers. "That's the second time you said that we're figuring this out. I don't know why you keep saying that? I'm more lost than ever."

Guardrail jumped in. "So, if you know what's going on, tell us. And can you also tell the limpin' chicken thank you for me? That she left the pickled eggs alone for a change. Come to think of it, Dixie, give me one of those bad boys."

Star smiled at the big motorcycle mechanic. "You just said thank you to her yourself. She knows, I can sense it."

Piper could wait no longer. "So, tell us, Star. What is going on?"

Star took a seat at Edith and Lily's table. She studied Piper and Ida at the next table, and then smiled at Edith and Lily. "Glad to see you both. It's been a while. I heard Lily had not been feeling well."

Lily tittered. "I'm fine, thank you, Star. Parts of the body just need a rest sometimes when you get to be my age."

Ida raised her eyebrows. "Well? You going to tell us, Star, or are we going to have to beat it out of you?"

Star drew a deep breath. "Alright. Dog's old Army buddy, Lugnut, died of a heart attack. I think. His spirit was holding his chest when it appeared in my shower. And I had a dream about a man having a heart attack. But that's not the worst of it. In my dream, he died of a heart attack induced by something a woman gave to him. But for some reason, Lugnut is also worried about Dog and his spirit is trying to send us a message. I don't think we figured it all out yet, but I'm sure it means that Dog may be in danger."

Ida huffed. "Dog? Why would anyone want to hurt Dog?"

Star shrugged. "I don't know. Like I said, we haven't

figured it all out yet. But we have to find out. We can't just sit around and wait for something to happen."

Dixie's voice blared over all the others. "I got to know. All these nicknames are getting on my nerves. Why can't we just call a man by his name?"

I raised one eyebrow. "Really, Dixie? With all this going on you're worried about nicknames?"

Dixie shrugged her shoulders at me. "It got stuck in my head. I want to know."

Digger surprised us all when he answered. "Some names just stick. Like mine."

Dixie looked at Digger sideways. "Are you messing with me? You dig graves. That's not rocket science. But Dog Breath? Lugnut?"

Dog's head was hung low, but he raised his chin a little and spoke. But not to us. It was like he was talking to a memory. "Lugnut got his name when he was a teenager. Worked on a pit crew for a race team based out of Statesboro. They raced at tracks all over the southeast. He was a tire changer and could take off five lug nuts, then zip in five new lug nuts in three and a half seconds. So, his nickname was a bit like Digger's. It was obvious and it just fit."

I should not have done it. The boys were pretty tight lipped about their nicknames. Almost like it was some sort of secret handshake. But, my curiosity made me speak. "How did you get the name Dog Breath?"

Dog glared at me for a moment with a mixture of surprise and confusion. "I haven't thought about that for a long time, Ginger. But in 'Nam, me and Lugnut worked long hours every day. We didn't get many days off. But when we got leave, we cut loose. More than we should've sometimes, but we were young. One time, I had a wicked hangover after a two day bender and a two-star general come into the motor pool for transport. When I spoke to him, he could tell I was hungover. He chewed me out for not being one hundred percent. As part of the scolding he gave me, he said I had breath that smelled worse than a dog's hind end. Lugnut overheard, and when the general left, he started teasing me about it. He would say I worked like a dog and had the breath to prove it. The others picked up on it and it just stuck. Lugnut wasn't even trying when he gave me the handle."

I could feel the heartache in his voice. He grieved for his lost friend and I was sorry I asked the question. "I'm sorry. That was insensitive for me to ask. I forgot Lugnut gave you your nickname."

Guardrail burped then blurted out. "It's alright, Ginger. We're all family here. Heck, I got my name from Dog. And I'm not proud of the story leading up to it. I was running with a bad crowd. But even though Dog was dealing with that PTPMS, or whatever they call it, that didn't stop him from helping me. I was going down the wrong road and he and his family set me straight. I owe a lot to Dog and his family."

Dog had tears in his eyes when he spoke. "We helped

each other, buddy. I was in bad shape and the PTSD almost drove me over the edge. I was hoping to find a way to fit back into society but it just didn't seem possible. Then when we started the motorcycle shop together, it was like I finally found a way to be a little normal again. It was my security blanket. And it happened because of you. You kept me on the right road, too, going in the right direction. You were acting like a guardrail for my life. Since then, you and your big heart have kept more people on the road going in the right direction during a good week than I have my whole life. You're a good man and the name Guardrail was a perfect choice for you."

Guardrail furrowed his brow. "You haven't told that story in a long time. But, boy, does that bring back some memories, and emotions." He punched Dog gently in the arm. "And that's for making me realize how old we are now."

I did not know what to do. The sensitive side of Dog and Guardrail was rarely on display in public. Fortunately, Dixie ended the moment. "Well, now that we're done with the Steel Magnolias minute, I'm not sure you will want that pickled egg you ordered."

My experience in the pub taught to pay attention when Dixie's voice had that tone of disbelief while talking about the pickled eggs. I spun to inspect the pickled egg jar. The sight would be surprising to most people, but I experienced enough in The Grumpy Chicken and knew to expect anything. The pickled egg jar was foaming and overflowing.

Star chuckled. "The chicken is happy that we were bonding, telling some personal stories. But, she is also concerned about Dog. It is unusual that a spirit feels it necessary to warn an old army pal just after his death. It's the Chicken's way of letting us know we need to focus and act before it's too late. We have to find out what happened to Lugnut. And we need to protect Dog."

Chapter Six

"Come on, Candy. Grease is about to start! You said you wanted to watch this." Slick hated the movie, but he wanted to keep her happy.

"I'll be right there. I need to finish my hair," Candy hollered from his small bathroom.

"Well, hurry up. I'm not made of money and I don't have one of those fancy beep boop machines that can pause or rewind live TV." Slick looked at his watch again and confirmed he was right. The movie started in three minutes.

"I'll be there in a minute. I hate when you make me hurry." Candy's voice squeaked as she yelled so he would hear her.

Slick rolled his eyes and headed into his efficiency. The refrigerator there may be small, but he kept it well stocked with beer. He threw open the fridge door and grabbed a cold one. The "phst" sound made when he worked the can's pop top was his favorite sound on earth. He took a long draw of cold beer, then wiped his mouth with his shirt sleeve.

Candy emerged from the bathroom. "Don't use your sleeve as a napkin. That is so…crude."

"What? It works and makes my shirt smell like beer. Win, win." Slick smiled when he finished.

"Men, I will never understand them."

"Whoa! Don't get me started on women. There isn't a man on the planet that understands them."

Candy smiled. "We like it that way. A bit of mystery never hurts. It helps to keep you men on your toes."

Slick smiled back. "Hey, this movie is starting. We gonna watch it or what?"

"Of course, silly." Candy strolled over to the plaid couch and plopped down in the center.

Slick followed, sat next to her, and put his arm around her. The opening credits rolled and music started to play. He noticed it made her happy. "There's that smile. I love when you smile."

"You're such a con artist. That sweet tongue of yours is going to get you into trouble sooner or later. But, what else do you like about me?"

Slick raised his eyebrows. "Um. Well, let's see. Your eyes. Yeah definitely your eyes."

Candy smiled in response. "And what else?"

Slick paused, then blurted out, "Your hair. You always have it fixed up so pretty."

Candy once again smiled at him. "You sweet talking fool. You better say my hair since I'm the best hairdresser in Statesboro. But, my hair is a mess right now, because you rushed me. I just threw it in a pony tail for now. I'm going to fix it up at the first commercial."

"You look fine, baby. Now, shhh. The credits are done. It's starting."

The two love birds cuddled on the couch and watched a young Olivia Newton-John and John Travolta ham it up. Slick took a quick break to run to the refrigerator and grab a second beer.

"Can't you wait until the commercial?" Candy pointed at the TV as she spoke.

"Nope. These beer cans just don't hold enough beer. I can still see the TV from the kitchenette." Slick retook his seat. He was quick and his spot was still nice and warm.

"See, I didn't miss a thing. Did you miss me?" He grinned like a smart aleck.

"Yeah. It smelled better for a minute while you were gone." She returned the know-it-all grin.

"I deserved that, I guess."

A commercial came on and Candy began to rise to go fix her hair, but she stopped on the edge of the couch cushion. "What is this. Did you get a new medication?"

"No. It's Lugnut's. I took it from his place." Slick's voice was choppy and he did not look at her.

Candy raised her eyebrows and huffed. "And why would you do that? Your poor friend just died and you take his heart medication? What's wrong with you?"

"I don't like the way this all happened. Something is not right. I know he had heart issues, but from what he told me the medicine made him healthier than when he was thirty. It was stupid of me, I just did it without thinking. I couldn't stop wondering if something went wrong with his pills and that's why he had the heart attack."

Candy's eyes melted and she put her hand on Slick's cheek. She studied him for a moment. "Honey, I know you and your Vietnam friends are tight. And that you worry about each other. It's very sweet. But, you have to face that you and your friends are getting older. Lugnut's heart just gave out. The doctors at the VA told him he was lucky to do as well as he did. That's what they said, right?"

Slick's eyes lowered and he looked at his beer can. "Yeah, I guess. But, it still doesn't feel right. And it really sucks!"

Candy smiled and winced at the same time. Slick was grieving and her heart ached for him. But a sweet man was exposed as the grief revealed his true self. It was beautiful and she felt joy at having him in her life. "I'm sorry. I shouldn't have been so blunt. But, I don't want you going off on some elaborate conspiracy thing."

Slick chuckled. "It's alright. I know you are right. And I'm not smart enough to come up with a conspiracy theory."

Candy snickered. "Don't sell yourself short. You were smart enough to get me."

He smiled and then kissed her. The commercial break ended and the movie resumed. "You missed your chance to finish your hair."

"It was worth it. I'll go the next commercial." She gave him another kiss and scooted back into the dent in the center cushion and settled in.

The movie followed the script they knew by heart. Candy lost count of how many times she watched this particular movie. It was one of her favorites, but watching with Slick made it perfect.

It is a sign of our modern times that commercials seem to get more air time than the show. So, it didn't take long until the next break.

"Here's my chance. Be right back." Candy popped up and ran to the bathroom.

Slick was putting it off. But, Candy was right. He had worked himself into a ball of nerves over Lugnut's death and it was silly. He needed to calm himself and let it go.

The oxygen was right next to the couch. He just picked up a fresh tank and it was full. With Candy in the bathroom, it was a good time to aerate his lungs. It would help calm his nerves and he hated when she saw him use the mask.

He hooked up the tube, connecting the mask to the tank. Then he checked to make sure everything was set up right. When he was sure it was, he turned the valve on and put the mask over his mouth and nose.

Candy loved fixing her hair and she wanted to look good for Slick. She spent an extra minute to get it just right. The wavy bob was being difficult today, but she coerced her hair into shape.

Once she was satisfied with the hairstyle, she brushed her teeth. She didn't want her breath to smell, either. Now, she felt presentable.

Candy walked like she was on a cat walk out into the living room. She screamed when she saw Slick. Slick's head had fallen onto the back of the couch and he was unconscious.

She checked his breathing, and there was none. She tried to find a pulse, again nothing. She started to cry as she took out her cell phone and dialed nine, one, one.

Chapter Seven

The decision had been made. It was clear we needed to find out what happened to Lugnut and why it involved Dog Breath. But, we couldn't agree who should go to Lugnut's funeral with Dog.

An informal meeting came to order and the debate began after everyone was served lunch. Piper as usual tried to moderate the discussion. "It's pretty simple. We need someone who knows how to investigate and ask the right questions. Like me."

Ida huffed. "Of course, you think you should go. But, Dog is going to an Army buddy's funeral. He will be spending time with the family, and they will be talking about the time in Vietnam. It might be better to send someone who understands what military families go through."

I pinched my lips and nodded in agreement, then asked, "Well, other than Dog, who has military experience."

Instinctively we all scanned the men in the room. We all knew Digger had served a few years in the navy, but it was not during war time and he spent most of his time pushing paper behind a desk. Guardrail never served. Dad spent time in the Army, but he was not the best choice to send into a sensitive situation. Hence, our dilemma.

Edith's voice surprised us all and I immediately felt guilty for being chauvinistic. Edith announced, "Dearies, just about every man in my family has served. My nephew is even currently stationed in Germany, in the Marines. Our dad was in the Army, WWII, and we attended more than one military funeral. I could go."

Lily added, "If you go, I should go, too."

"No, you've been sick and still need to rest. I can go and help Dog, you stay here and get better." Edith glared at her sister to make it clear. Lily was not coming with her.

Lily nodded in agreement. She knew traveling and sleeping in a strange bed would be hard on her.

Star emerged from the restroom and looked more like herself. Her hair was neatly brushed and styled and she wore a clean, pretty blouse and jeans. She even smiled as she sat down to eat her hamburger. "I'm certain that Lugnut's spirit didn't know how to communicate with us and panicked. The poor ghost dogged me all day trying to figure it out and is now relieved that we finally got his message. I should have known sooner. It is hard for some right after they pass to the other side. They are disoriented and don't how to do even the simplest of things."

I put my hands on my hips and stared at Dog. "I think you should take Star, too. She has been the one communicating with Lugnut's spirit and it's important to keep that line of communication open. She may even sense something once she is there, around Lugnut's family and friends."

Dog nodded yes. "I agree. With all that has happened, we're just starting to understand the events of the past couple of days. There's still much to do and Star is the only one who can communicate with Lugnut."

"So, it's agreed. Dog will go to Statesboro with Edith and Star." I scanned the faces for objections. When, I came to Guardrail, he scowled at me.

"Ginger, you know there is no way I'm letting my best buddy and business partner go through this without me. I'm going too." Guardrail glared at me to underline it was not open to debate.

Dog picked his head up and cracked a small grin at Guardrail, then said, "Thanks. I can't imagine going through this without ya."

Ida added. "I can reserve a couple of hotel rooms for you, and whatever else you need to make the arrangements for the trip."

Dog turned to Ida. "That is very kind. Thank you. And if it wouldn't be too much to ask, can you have flowers sent using that laptop of yours, too?"

Ida nodded. "Sure. If you give me your credit card number. I'll help, but I'm not paying for flowers."

Guardrail threw his head back. "Oh boy! Here we go. I don't think I have ever seen Dog's credit card. I don't know if he even has one, let alone know the number."

Dog glared at his best friend hurt. "Are you saying I am cheap?"

Guardrail shook his head no and answered in a soft voice that sounded odd from such a big man. "I'm not saying anything. I should have just kept my mouth shut. Sorry."

Dog reached into his pocket and removed a blue cloth trifold wallet. I heard the sound of the Velcro unzipping and he took out a credit card. Then he held it in a way so that all could see. "Here ya go. No lilies. He didn't like them after going to too many of his friends' funerals. No offense, Lily." Dog glanced over to her table to make sure she understood. Then he continued, "He wanted his funeral to be a celebration. Get something with roses. He loved Guns 'n Roses." Then he left his stool and walked over to Ida, handing her the credit card.

Ida smiled at Dog, and took the card. "I'll make sure Lugnut gets something real nice. And I'll even make sure to dig up some online coupons and save you a few bucks."

"Thanks. I appreciate it. I appreciate how nice you all have been to me." Dog glanced around the bar, to each of his friends. He meant what he said...we felt it. Then he cracked the slightest smile for all to see, to emphasize how much we meant to him.

It didn't last long. Beth entered the pub like a child visiting Disney World for the first time, moving slow and with purpose to take it all in while containing her excitement. She must have heard something had happened. She tittered, then said, "So it's true, something transpired with your detestable chicken ghost. I heard a rumor. It's the only reason you would all be assembled here now. And I can see it on your faces"

Piper answered with a slight growl in her voice. "What you see on our faces is mourning and concern. Dog's best friend from Vietnam just died."

"Oh, I am sorry to hear that. They say the bonds formed between the soldiers over there was unbreakable." Beth tried to flash Dog a compassionate expression, but it just came off as smug.

"Thanks, Beth. But, you can never understand what we went through over there. Nobody can unless they were there. So, don't even try."

The pub fell quiet. Dog was back to his cranky old self and I was unsure what to do or say. But I didn't need to do a thing. Dad burst through the kitchen door into the solemn scene. He skimmed the room and said, "What's with all the long faces. So, a war buddy died. I can tell ya, this is not how you deal with it. Every good soldier would want you to have a few beers and some good belly laughs to remember his life. Now, let's lose the gloom and doom and celebrate the man's life." Dad went to the tap, poured himself a beer and took a sip. Then he noticed the drip tray was a mess and proceeded to clean it.

Dog actually smiled. It was genuine and even had a bit of relief to it. "Now there's a man who understands. Lugnut would never want me to mope or be sad. He always said to enjoy the day and get as much out of it as you can. Each twenty-four hours is a gift. And he was right. Dixie, a round of your best beer for me and my friends."

Dixie stared at Dog like he was an alien. Then she snorted and picked up three mugs. "You got it, but what did you mean by our best beer. You and your amigos always drink the cheapest lager on tap."

"Well, that's because we consider it to be your best beer!" Dog pointed at the tap indicating to Dixie he wanted the beers now.

Ida chimed in once again. "Hey, you know I can do some digging on my computer. See what was going on with Lugnut just before he died. Maybe that will help to figure out what is going on."

Guardrail made a face. "I just kind of assumed you and Piper would do that anyway."

Piper was frowning. "I still think I should go, but I can help Ida do some background checks. Sure"

I sighed. "So, we have a plan, sort of. What are you going to do when you get there, Dog?"

Dog studied his shoes for a moment, then said, "I think I will do just like we did over in 'Nam. We'll do exactly what is necessary for the moment. There is no use looking too far into the future and making plans that will likely be derailed after the first shot."

"That is… pessimistic." Dixie was trying to be nice, I could tell, but she could have chosen her words better.

"I understand, Dog. With the first shot fired, all plans go to hell in a hand basket." Dad didn't even look up from the drip tray he was cleaning.

Dog nodded in agreement and took a long sip from his fresh beer. Wartime rules were brutal, you did what you needed to do to survive. And it concerned me that Dog thought he needed to revert to the means and methods he learned in Vietnam.

Chapter Eight

"Come on, I dropped off the luggage with the valet. Time to go to the funeral home." Dog seemed to be operating on some sort of autopilot.

"We got plenty of time. Lugnut isn't going anywhere. Guardrail wanted to get us checked into our rooms before we headed over." Edith had an odd mix of compassion and frustration to her tone.

Guardrail walked back to the group and handed Star a card key. "You and Edith will be sharing a room, and Dog and me are in the one right next door."

Star took the plastic card and put it in her pocket. "I hope Ida requested double beds."

Guardrail shuddered. "I better go ask at the desk before we leave and make sure. There is no way I am sleeping in a bed with Dog." He made a beeline back to the front desk.

Star studied the hotel lobby. The morning was spent driving out to Statesboro and the only thing she had sensed for the last few hours was Dog's immense sadness. Now, out of the car she could let her paranormal abilities breath a little. But, most of what she sensed was still Dog. His sorrow was deep and she realized Dog was trying to be strong in front of his friends.

Star took up a spot next to Dog Breath. "How are you doing? You seem a little zoned out."

Dog locked eyes with her. "I'm going to bury a man who I went to war with. A man I thought I might die with while out in the swamp and jungle or even during a weekend pass. You don't know how it was. A shoe shine boy could detonate a bomb while shining your shoes. Or a grieved widow could throw a hand grenade into a crowd of soldiers. It was that simple over there. If it was your time, it was your time. We lost a lot of our friends, but Lugnut, Slick, and me made it back. Now, in a flash, Lugnut is gone."

Star pinched her lips and sighed. "I know. It's hard to lose someone you care about. But, it is part of life. And it should make you feel better to know he loved you, too. His spirit sought a way to warn you, and just after passing to the other side. That is very unusual and only someone who cared deeply would do that."

Dog cracked a small smile. "Don't forget he found a way to see you in the shower. Lugnut and Slick could never control themselves around the pretty ladies."

Star blushed and was surprised she was also a bit angry. This shower incident was going to stay with her. She was sure more jokes about it were in the future and she had to find a way to deal with them.

Edith understood that Star was uncomfortable with the

teasing and came to the rescue. "When was the last time you saw Lugnut's family?"

"Last summer. He got tickets to the race track in Myrtle Beach. Me, Slick, and Lugnut had a boy's weekend up at the beach. But, we did spend a day here in Statesboro to visit family."

Guardrail returned shaking his head. "Ida may know how to hack into a database, but she sure didn't know how to book a hotel room. We had two rooms with queen beds. I got it changed. I need that card key back, Star."

Star swapped keys with the big man, then he lumbered back to the front desk while muttering, "Ida has some splaining to do when we get back."

Edith snorted. "Well, at least he caught it. I should tell you now, Star. I snore."

Star rolled her eyes and folded her arms. "And here I thought this trip might a nice change of pace. You know, get away from Potter's Mill for a few days."

Dog laughed. "You can have Guardrail then. But, I should warn you, he snores like he talks, loud and often."

Guardrail returned and waved at the other three to follow as he headed to the front door. "Rooms are all set. So, time to go pay our respect."

They piled into the rental car and drove over to the funeral home. Guardrail drove and Star did her best to relay the directions off her cell phone, but tech was not her thing. At least she knew how to use the GPS and that was better than Edith or Dog Breath. Eventually, they found their way without too much trouble.

The funeral home was large and beautiful. The entire site was immaculate and the landscaping perfect and green. The building was impressive, painted white with black trim. Everything looked new and fresh, even the burgundy awning over the bricked front walk leading to the main entrance.

Dog got out of the car and gave the place the once over. "Looks like Lugnut is going out in style. Good. He deserves it.'

The four approached the front door and entered. The door was not even fully closed when Lugnut's widow, Bianca Howard, welcomed them. "Dog! So nice to see you. I was hoping you would come early. You must have left Potter's Mill at the crack of dawn to get here by now."

"Nothing is too much trouble to come and help you out. Glad to be here." Dog gave her a hug.

Star and Edith flashed each other a quick look with jaws hanging. Dog never showed emotion openly and this display surprised them.

Dog let Bianca go and took a step back. "I should introduce you to my friends. They came to provide support. This is Guardrail, who you know already. And this is Star, and that is Edith."

All three nodded their heads to say hello as they heard their names.

Bianca extended her hand to shake. "Pleased to meet you all." After the formalities, Bianca sniffled and wiped her nose with a handkerchief. "This is a lot for me to deal with. But, I am glad to see you, Dog. Lugnut loved and missed you. He would say that you and Slick knew him better than he knew himself. So, I am sure he is happy you are here. I'm happy, too."

"Can't say I am happy to be here like this. But, I wanted to be here. That's for sure. To help you in any way we can." Dog pinched his eyebrows to share his sincerity with her.

"You're such a sweet man, Dog. I needed a little ray of sunshine like you today." Lugnut's widow smiled, weakly, to show her thanks.

Edith could not resist. She turned to Star and whispered. "Is she talking about the same Dog Breath we know? I never heard anyone call him a ray of sunshine."

Star shrugged in response.

Dog scanned the large room and asked, "Hey, where is Slick?"

Bianca's face went white and she fumbled for words. She finally managed to say, "You didn't hear?"

Dog shrugged, "No. Hear what?"

Bianca drew in a deep breath. "It happened last night. Slick got a bad tank of oxygen. It almost killed him. He's in the hospital."

Dog slumped like he took a blow to the stomach. "You've got to be kidding me? How can that be?"

Bianca shook her head. "I have no idea. But, Candy, his most recent girlfriend, called and told me late last night. She was so worried about not being here this morning. But she insisted on being at Slick's side at the VA hospital. Like I said, I have had a lot to deal with the last couple of days."

Guardrail noticed the impact this news had on Dog and asked, "How far is this hospital from here? Maybe we can go see Slick later today?"

Bianca shrugged, "I don't know, forty-five minutes maybe."

Guardrail turned to ask Dog when he wanted to leave. But all he saw was the hind end of his business partner going out the front door.

Edith gently grabbed Guardrail's forearm, and with some effort, and tugged at him to stay. "Let him have some alone time. He's lost one of his best friends and just learned another is lucky to be alive in the hospital. He can use a minute."

Guardrail looked at the old spinster, confused. He knew Dog for many years, but this news seemed to suck all the life out of him. "I'm going to get him. He is my

best friend and I need to be there for him." And with
that he left.

Five minutes passed and Star, Edith, and Bianca were
now chatting like lifelong friends when they spotted
Guardrail once again. He was staring at the ground
muttering to himself.

Star asked, "Is everything alright?"

Guardrail shook his head. "No. Dog is gone. I looked
all over the parking lot and around the building. But I
can't find him. I think he left and went somewhere.
What I don't know, is why would he do that?"

Star closed her eyes and opened herself to the chatter
of the other side. She searched for Dog's sorrow, trying
to find him. Then she opened her eyes and said, "I think
you're right Guardrail. He is gone. I can't sense his
sorrow anymore."

Bianca glanced at Star sideways. "What was that?
And what did you mean? You some kind of spirit
whisperer?"

Star smiled. "I never heard it put that way. But, yes, I
can communicate with the spirit world. I own a new age
shop in Potter's Mill and do readings most of the time."

Bianca fussed with her hands and confusion flashed
across her face. She finally asked, "Is it improper to
ask? But I would like to know if you can talk to loved
ones that have just passed."

Star formed a small, compassionate smile. "But, of

course. And if you are referring to Lugnut, I have already seen his spirit once."

Guardrail blurted out without thinking, "Yeah, and he saw plenty of you, too!" Then he blushed when he saw Bianca, Lugnut's widow, staring at him perplexed. He added, "It's a long story, I tell it to ya later, when it's more appropriate."

Star glared back at him with gritted teeth. This teasing was going to test her patience. Then she composed herself and said, "That was uncalled for, thank you very much Mr. Guardrail. But, you are missing the urgent 'to do' item on our list. We need to find Dog."

Guardrail frowned. "You're right, Star. And the only place he has to go is the hotel. So, maybe we should head back there to see if we can find him."

To everyone's surprise, the next person who spoke was Bianca. "He may be going to the VA hospital, too. To see Slick."

Edith added, "Looks like a wild goose chase just started. And we ain't the goose. So, we best be going and get to the chasing."

With that, Edith, Star, and Guardrail said goodbye and left to find Dog.

Chapter Nine

The crowd in the Grumpy Chicken was light, and it was a good thing. Star was on the phone, and as usual things were not going to plan. "No, I'm not kidding, we're looking for Dog right now. We think he might have headed off for the local hospital." I noticed Star's voice sounded tired.

I listened to the whole story, and somehow it didn't surprise me. Living in The Grumpy Chicken with Dad must have taught me to roll with the punches, even when things get stranger than normal. "So, it feels like Ida, Piper, and I have sat this one out long enough. But I'm not sure what's the best thing for us to do."

Star snorted on the other end of the phone. "We could use you here in Statesboro. We need to look into the heart attack that happened to Lugnut, but now we also have the bad oxygen that almost killed Dog's other friend, Slick. It's too much of a coincidence and I keep getting the feeling that Lugnut's ghost is about to make another appearance. The spirit world is unsettled."

"I hear ya. Lugnut's heart attack followed by his ghost in your shower was a warning. I understand your assessment of that. And now this other friend from

Vietnam has something weird happen. That seems like too much of a coincidence."

Star paused, then added, "Yes, and … "

I heard the rustling noises and then Edith's voice came over the phone. "We can do all the analyzing and theorizing you girls want when you get here. But we need two teams here in Statesboro. Get your pretty little bottom moving, missy. We need you here to investigate the Slick guy while we try and find Dog. And that still leaves investigating the odd occurrences surrounding Lugnut's death."

I heard more rustling. Guardrail's voice suddenly boomed from the receiver and I had to hold it a couple of inches from ear. "We talked about things here and there is no way we can cover all the bases. Edith is right. You need to get moving. When can you be here? I need to be able to focus on finding my buddy."

I took a deep breath. "Let me talk to Ida and Piper. We will get on the road as fast as possible. It's only noon, and I think we should be able to get there before dinner time."

"Alright. Sounds good. Now, I got to go and find Dog. Bye." With that the call ended and I realized Dad was staring at me.

"I guess you overheard. I need to go to Statesboro and help Edith, Star, and Guardrail find Dog. He's missing, but they think he may have gone to visit another friend who had an accident and is in the hospital."

Dad huffed and folded his arms. "Guess that is to be expected. Something bizarre is always happening and no one ever sits still around here."

I chuckled. "What would you have us do? Ignore the events and not help our friends when they need it?"

Dad grimaced. "You make it sound soooooo like the right thing to do when you say it like that."

"It is the right thing to do." The smile crept over my face even though I didn't want it to. I was afraid Dad might think I was being smug.

His eyes darted around. "I know. I just miss my little girl when she's gone."

I melted and went over to hug my father. "It will be a quick trip. You won't even have time to miss me. I can't be gone too long. You sneak more beer than you should without me nagging you to watch your health."

"I didn't think of the extra beer, that is good." Dad tried to smile, but the coy face gave him away.

"Well, don't drink too much beer. I'm asking Dixie and Bones to keep an eye on you while I'm gone."

Dixie came out though the swinging door from the kitchen. "I heard my name. Did I get a raise?"

The laugh just slipped out of me. "Not exactly. It's more like more responsibility. I need you to keep an eye on Dad. I need to head for Statesboro with Ida and Piper for a bit."

Ida glared back at me. "I hate when I have to watch Tom's beer consumption. He always threatens to fire me."

"He doesn't mean it. You both know it. But he needs to limit how much he drinks. It's bad for his health and I need you to help me take care of him."

Dixie shrugged and held her hands up in defeat. "I feel like …"

"I should go, too." I almost forgot Digger was sitting at the end of the bar, alone, when he raised his voice and interrupted. "I'm not sitting here any longer drinking beer by myself while Dog and Guardrail are gone."

The sound of breaking glass made me flinch. But there was a low, thud at the same time. It happened so fast, I could not figure out what it was.

Dixie howled. "Son of a malted turd! Digger's beer exploded!"

Dad was standing near Digger when it happened and I saw him checking himself for injuries. But it appeared that he was fine.

Digger checked, too. But he was not so lucky. He clutched a wound over his left eye with both hands. I was surprised, and so was everyone else when he spoke. "I guess the grumper doesn't like my idea!"

Dad was still white and muttered. "You might be more right than you know."

I grabbed a wet towel and tried to tend to Digger. He grabbed the cloth and moaned when pressing it to the cut. "That sure doesn't feel like it's going to help my good looks."

Dixie chuckled. "I wouldn't worry. Maybe it will improve things. You got to stay positive."

Digger glared with the one good eye he had left. "You saying I'm ugly."

Dixie shrugged. "Just trying to keep things light. No offense intended."

I had no time for nonsense and cut them off. "Come on, Digger. I'll take you to see Doc. If you need some stitches, he can patch you up. Dixie, can you call Ida and Piper and tell that we need to go to Statesboro, now. Ask them to get ready and pick me and Digger up at Doc's."

Dad scanned the bar. "Sure, leave me and Bones here alone."

"I'm not taking Dixie. She just needs to make a few calls. And I saw you check the place, just like I did. So, we both know it's dead in here and you'll be fine."

"Dixie, can you make the calls?" I was surprised at the agitation in my voice.

Dixie frowned at me and nodded yes. "You never think I should go on one of these junkets. You know, I can help. It would be nice to be out of the pub once in a while."

Bones wandered out of the kitchen and came through the swinging door. "I hate hearing everything all by myself in the back. And I have opinions, too. Take her instead of Ida." He pointed at Dixie. "Since Ida took a time out with Scooter so he could go shoot episodes in Europe, she's been a bit of a, um, scatterbrain."

I knew he was right. Ida was depressed and not at her best with the current break in her relationship. "You know what, you're right. Think you can hold this place down with just you and Dad?"

Bones nodded in the affirmative. Dad was getting his wits back and barked at me. "You just can't resist dumping the workload on me, can ya?"

"There isn't much to do, and if you need help, call Ida. She can help you if she has to." I raised my eyebrows to let Dad know I was not going to change my mind.

Dad huffed. "Fine. At least she'll let me drink as much beer as I want."

"Don't be difficult with her. She is touchy right now with things being rocky with Scooter. Be considerate."

Dad laughed. "She *is* a tough one and the last thing I want is to stand in for her boyfriend if she feels she needs to vent."

I chuckled. "I knew you understand better than you let on."

Dixie hurriedly threw off her apron and grabbed her coat. "Do I still need to call Piper?"

"Well unless you got a new car that I don't know about, yeah. Piper is the only one of us with a decent car." I helped Digger to his feet and we headed to the door.

Dixie fumbled in her jeans pocket and pulled out her phone.

I glanced back to Bones and hollered. "Can you make sure that mess where Digger was sitting is clean?'

Bones snickered. "Sure. No problem. I have lots of experience cleaning up a beer explosion by a ghost chicken."

Dixie looked up from the cell phone, turned and scolded Bones over her shoulder. "Don't be a smarty pants. And I have cleaned way more unusual things in this place."

I heard Bones try to whisper to Dad, but his voice carried. "I think she's forgetting a few things and underestimates me."

Dixie glanced at me and smiled, then whispered, "He still has a lot to learn."

I nodded. "Yep. Now let's get Digger back together so we can get a move on to Statesboro and help Dog with all of this."

Chapter Ten

Dog Breath leaned forward so the cabbie could hear him. "Keep the meter running and wait here, I will be back in about ten minutes."

With a quick check of every window, Dog made his way around the small, one story ranch. In the back, he found an unlocked window. He opened it all the way.

Slowly and carefully, Dog climbed in through the open window since he thought he heard voices inside. Slick's accident made no sense to him. He needed to look around his house for a clue or anything that looked unusual.

The entry point dropped the not so stealthy motorcycle mechanic into Slick's den. It was clean and meticulously organized and Dog expected no less. Slick worked in motor pool office in Vietnam, and once he returned home found similar work behind a desk as administrator. And he knew how to keep things neat and organized.

The books and bug specimens caught Dog's eye. One of the things that intrigued Slick over in Vietnam was the insects. Some were huge and bizarre and he wanted to know more about them. He began to study them and developed a fascination with the small creatures. His love of insects may have developed overseas, but he brought it home and was always trying to learn more about them.

A quick scan of the den told Dog Breath that this room was not going to provide any clues, so he moved on. He still heard the voices. But now he could tell it was a radio left on in the bedroom, probably an alarm playing news for no one.

In the living room, he made a beeline for the coffee table and found a pill bottle. He picked it up and read the label, but it confused him. The prescription was for Harry Campbell. What was Lugnut's heart medication doing in Slick's house?

He pocketed the bottle, and while doing so, it jumped out at him. A small green gas tank. "Bingo, and the hose is still hooked up." Dog smiled since he knew this was the tank that must have put Slick in the hospital.

After quickly coiling the small length of hose around the valve, Dog picked up the tank and power walked to the front exit. He may have come in through a window, but he was in a hurry now and the front door was the fastest way back to his cab.

He closed the front door and made sure it latched, then he hurried back to the cab. However, the cabbie saw him coming and jumped out of the car. He held his hand up like a traffic cop signaling stop. "You're not getting in my cab with that thing."

Dog looked down at the green tank in his arms and

paused. Then he looked the cabbie in the eye. "I have a medical condition and need oxygen. It's safe and a doctor prescribed it for me. It's not a problem."

The cabbie eyed him. "I thought you said you were from out of town?"

Dog once again paused. "Well, I am. But my buddy was holding my tank for me. But I need it today. It was an emergency. That is why I couldn't wait for my friends to drive me and took a cab so they could stay at the funeral home."

The wary cabbie studied him from the side of his face. "It looks dangerous to me."

Sensing he almost had the cautious cabbie's consent to bring the tank, Dog decided he needed to do one last thing to convince the driver. So, he put the mask on and cracked the valve. "See there's nothing to worr…" Dog collapsed unconscious onto the sidewalk.

***

The nurse fluffed his pillow and smiled. "Glad to see you awake. Your vitals are coming back, too."

"How long have I been here?" Dog tried to sit up while he spoke.

"Only about a half hour."

"I had a green tank and some pills in my pocket. They are really important and may be key evidence in a murder." Dog was trying to find his pants while pleading with the nurse.

"Calm down, all your possessions are safe."

His head was groggy and he felt like he'd been hit by an NFL linebacker. But then a thought overwhelmed him and he glanced around the room, looking for something that told him what hospital he was in. "What hospital is this? I was looking for the VA facility."

The nurse smiled. "Why, silly, this is the VA hospital. Your cab driver said you talked about your Vietnam friends and he knew you were a vet. And this was the closest hospital. So, he brought you here. We checked your wallet and confirmed your service."

"Well, I am a Vietnam vet, that's true." Dog had a pounding headache and rubbed his temples. "I never caught a break, but maybe, just maybe. Is there a Slick…I'm sorry. Is there an Eric Cooke registered here?"

The nurse looked at him puzzled. "That's a bit odd to ask after a near death experience, but why do you want to know?"

"It's important, and more people may be in danger. I think someone may have committed murder, and is trying to kill others." Dog pleaded with his eyes.

"I can check. In the meantime, get some rest. You don't seem to understand you were just about dead when the cabbie brought you in here." Then she turned and left.

The nurse returned in a couple of minutes and she stood at the end of the bed and folded her arms. "How did you know Eric was here?"

Dog stared out the window and couldn't look her in the eye. "It was his gas that knocked me out. I suspected that someone may have tried to hurt him with the oxygen he used. But the cabbie didn't want the tank in his car. I thought a small whiff wouldn't hurt me. But when I took a sniff to show the driver it was safe to take in the cab, well, next thing I wake up here."

"You're lucky you didn't die."

"And so was Slick. That's what we call Eric. And that's why I need to see him. I think someone tried to kill him. I must see him. What room is he in?"

"You are in no shape to walk anywhere. And we still don't know what happened to you. Well, you confirmed the oxygen tank part of the story, your account is just like the cabbie's. I better get that tank secured and have it checked for what is in it."

Dog scooted up toward the headboard and tried to sit up slightly. "I need to go see Slick. Is there any way I can go see him now?"

"Well, I guess I could bring you in a wheelchair."

Dog Breath clapped his hands together in delight, but then he grabbed his forehead. "Wow, this headache is brutal." He then tried to smile as a sign of thanks. "A wheelchair will work. Let's go, and put it on my bill."

The nurse chuckled. "Oh, we bill for everything, trust me. As for seeing your friend, you seem genuinely worried about something. So, I will take you, but I want security to accompany us. I have no idea what's going on here, but the one thing I am sure of, this all very unusual."

"That's just fine. In fact, we may need to call the police before this is done. Oh, and one more thing. Can you test those pills in my pants pocket to see if they were tampered with or poisoned?"

The nurse threw her hands in the air. "There you go again! That is downright weird to ask something like that."

"I had heart pills for Lugnut, I mean Harry Campbell in my pocket. They need to be tested. I suspect someone replaced his pills and murdered him."

The nurse cocked her head. "Harry Campbell? That name sounds familiar. And he just died?"

Dog sighed. "Yeah, his heart went suddenly. It's why I suspect the pills."

"I can have the lab analyze the pills. But that will have to wait."

"No, it needs to happen *now*. We have no time; can we drop the pills off at the lab on the way to see Slick?"

The nurse refolded her arms. "A little bossy for a new patient, I can see you're going to be a handful."

"It's important."

She studied Dog for a moment. "I will have an orderly take the pills down with a request to analyze them. "

Dog sighed and his head drooped a bit in relief. "I can't thank you enough."

"I'm only doing this because you said others might be in danger. So, hold your thanks. I still have no idea which end is up with you." She slowly turned to the door. "I'll go get a wheelchair and a VA police officer. Then, we can go see Eric."

"Slick, no one calls him Eric!"

The nurse barked back. "It says Eric Cook on our registry. So as far as I'm concerned, it's Eric."

She left, but returned promptly pushing a wheelchair, and with an officer in tow. Dog made use of the short time and labored to sit up on the edge of the bed. When the nurse entered, he was holding the hospital gown shut with one hand behind his back. "Can I get something a little more like real clothes?"

The nurse checked the wheelchair to make sure it was ready to use. "That is standard issue, soldier. And no one will give you a second look, everyone is accustomed to it in here. Now, let's load you up."

With some effort she managed to get Dog Breath into the chair. "Well, it looks like we're ready to roll, Mr. Bell. Hold on."

"Call me Dog Breath."

The nursed laughed and rolled Dog out of the room. The VA hospital was huge and after fifteen minutes, the nurse said. "We're almost there, just a couple of rooms to go."

Dog was lost and there was no way he would have found Slick's room on his own. Plus, his head felt light and he had no strength in his legs. The nurse was right, his wheelchair ride worked out for the best in more ways than one.

The nurse turned into a hospital room and Dog saw Slick in a reclining bed that was raised so he could sit. Next to him sat a pretty woman, about the same age as Slick.

"Dog Breath! You are the last man I expected to see in here today." Slick smiled broadly.

"Slick, good to see you, too. But I have to say, you've looked better." Dog tried to smile but it was harder than he expected.

Slick chuckled. "I could say the same thing about you. But looks like your sad state got you a pretty lady to push you up here."

The nurse glared at Slick. "I'll have you know, I have two graduate degrees, so watch it."

Slick smiled at the nurse, then studied the VA police officer. "Seems like you must be a VIP in here, since you got a police escort."

Candy was trying to be polite, but lost her patience and cleared her throat, loudly. Slick took the hint. "Where are my manners. Dog, this is Candy. Candy this is Dog Breath."

Candy batted her eyes. "Nice to finally meet you. Slick has talked about you and Lugnut quite a bit."

Dog nodded his head slightly. "Nice to meet you, too, Candy. But I must apologize. We don't have a lot of time for pleasantries. We have too much to talk about, like what happened to you and Lugnut, and me."

Chapter Eleven

"Will you stop. We're almost there. What is it with older men? They have to go pee every ten minutes." Dixie rolled her eyes then leaned her head back on the seat. She was sitting in the back of the car, next to Digger.

"I have had to go for an hour now. And I really, *really* need to go now." Digger was sweating from the effort to hold it.

"Look, there's the funeral home. We are there." I was riding shotgun, busy with the GPS and trying to keep the peace. Piper's driving was more aggressive since we went to one wrong funeral parlor while Digger begged for a bathroom, and Dixie is, well, Dixie.

Dixie was the first to pop out of the car when we parked. It seemed like it hadn't even stopped when she opened the door. The rest of us unloaded and Piper stared down Dixie. "You needed to get out of the car I guess?"

Dixie blushed. "With all the pee talk, I have to go now, too."

We made for the front door and I was apprehensive

about crashing a wake where none of us knew anyone. Once inside, we were greeted by a sign informing us that Lugnut's wake was in the Monticello Room.

Dixie and Digger made for the rest rooms. And Piper provided an answer to the question rattling around in my head. How were we going to explain our arrival to a grieving family?

She was in journalist mode and took control. She led me further into the fancy place and we made our way to the Monticello Room. The crowd was light and most were standing, milling about. After shaking a few hands and introducing ourselves, Piper approached a woman in scrubs, "Hello, my name is Piper. We're friends of Dog Breath and came to help anyway we can. We were hoping to talk with Bianca Howard. Do you know where she is?"

The woman smiled broadly in reply. "No. But, my name is Linzi. I'm a nurse at the VA hospital where Lugnut was being treated. Maybe I can help you. I have known Lugnut for years."

Piper tilted her head back slightly. "Were you involved with treating his heart condition?"

Linzi nodded. "Of course. It was the reason Lugnut came to the hospital. Other than his ticker, he was in good health. It was so sad to see it fail on him."

I couldn't resist participating in the conversation. "My name is Ginger. Nice to meet you."

Linzi dropped her jaw and her eyes widened. "You're the one with the haunted pub, aren't you? The one who solves those unusual murders."

I smiled a little to be polite. "Yes, I'm that Ginger." It was a bit uncomfortable and I caught Piper rolling her eyes.

"Lugnut and Slick talked about the adventures Dog had with you. So nice to meet you." Linzi extended her hand to shake.

To be gracious, I shook it. "Would you know if there were any recent changes in the heart medication for Lugnut? It seemed like something changed according to his family and friends. They all felt it was a shock and kind of sudden."

Linzi shook her head no, and the smile on her face disappeared. "Not that I know."

Piper was studying the nurse. "Would you know where Bianca is, or if she's coming tonight?"

Linzi shrugged. "Well, the wake started earlier today, and there was one viewing at noon that lasted until three. But I couldn't make that one, I had to work. So, I came to this one that just started at five. She wasn't here when I got here, so no. I'm guessing she might show a little later, after a little break. She has been through a lot, including the first viewing."

Dixie came bounding into the room and made her way over to us. "That's so much better. So, what are we doing?"

Piper frowned at her. "We were having a conversation with Linzi here. Linzi, this is Dixie. Dixie, Linzi."

Dixie blushed. "Nice to meet you, Linzi. I didn't mean to interrupt."

I tried to continue. "Do you know what heart medication Lugnut was on?"

Linzi's face went blank. "I have to be honest. All these questions about Lugnut's medical condition are making me uncomfortable. Can we talk about something else?"

Piper didn't miss a beat. "Sure. Do you know anyone who would want to hurt Lugnut?"

Linzi flashed a nervous grin. "If I didn't know better, I would say you are investigating a murder."

I knew Piper's tone was a bit blunt, and jumped in. "Not really. But like I said, it seemed sudden and it surprised everyone. So, we do have questions."

Linzi eyed me while she searched for her words. "If you want to investigate something, I overheard Slick and Lugnut mention a top-secret mission they were involved with in 'Nam. Lugnut even mentioned to me that he needed to keep a low profile, because of it. When I asked what that meant, he clammed up."

Piper once again took control. "Well, that is very helpful, thank you. But it seems unusual for a nurse to know all that about a patient."

Linzi's nervous grin became a smile. "Oh, didn't I mention it? Lugnut and I dated before he married Bianca. Like I said, I have known him for a long time."

Dixie snorted. "Well, isn't that all nice and cozy."

As I was about to chide Dixie, Piper stopped me by saying, "Well, that is unusual. Was there any bad blood between you and Bianca?"

Linzi pinched her lips and quipped. "That's a bit personal. I think we're done here. You ladies have a nice day." She turned and strolled off.

Digger wandered over to us as Linzi walked away. "I see you're already making friends. She didn't look happy."

Piper shot back, "That is just it, Digger. For someone who dated the dead guy, she didn't seem too interested in him. And she was too perky."

Digger pointed to a woman in black talking to two others. "That is Bianca over there. I ran into her by accident as she came into the room. I think that's the woman we wanted to talk to, right?"

We all looked a Digger in shock. Dixie summed it up. "Well, luck is sometimes better than skill."

Piper gestured towards the widow. "Well, we came to talk to her. So, let's go talk to her."

The four of us exchanged quick glances when Dixie spoke again. "Don't you think the four of us descending on her might be a bit much?"

My eyebrows spiked. "That is actually a good though. I had no idea you could be so perceptive."

Dixie shrugged. "I tend bar. You learn how to read people and how to say hello. It is obvious a grieving widow wouldn't want to be ambushed by the four of us asking questions."

Piper nodded in agreement. "I agree. It's a good call to split up. Dixie, Digger, you two go talk with the other vets that are here. Ask about what Dog and Lugnut did over in Vietnam. There are a few old army buddies here and they're easy to spot. One is even wearing a VA hospital bracelet. They might know if Dog Breath and his friends did more than change oil during the war."

Digger grunted. "I never knew you had telescopic vision. How did you spot all that?"

"I just paid attention when we came in. Now go on. Ginger and I need to go talk to Bianca."

With that we split. Piper and I locked eyes as we approached Bianca, and we both understood this was more complex than we anticipated.

"Mrs. Campbell. We are so sorry for your loss. We came from Potter's Mill to see if we can do anything to help. We're friends of Dog Breath and heard that he's now missing." My thin voice revealed how my heart ached for her loss.

Bianca cracked a small, gracious smile. "Dog seems to have a lot of friends. There were a few of his other friends here earlier. But they're off looking for him now. That Guardrail guy was huge."

I smiled back at her. "He is big, but his heart is bigger. They were the ones who called us and filled us in. And asked that we come here to help."

"That is so kind of you." She studied Piper and me.

"I'm sorry. I am Ginger. And this Piper."

Bianca tilted her head to one side. "Lugnut mentioned you. He said you two were very smart and solved some pretty weird murders."

Piper looked like she had just learned aliens really did land in Roswell. "He mentioned me? I thought everyone just talked about Ginger and the ghost chicken."

Bianca chuckled. "Oh, he mentioned the ghost chicken, too. It's kind of hard to ignore that."

Piper regathered her composure. "I was hoping we would run into you. Dog told us that this all happened so suddenly. Did you notice anything unusual with Lugnut before it happened?"

"No not really. But I wasn't focused on finding anything. We were just living our lives. But, when

Slick got that bad oxygen, that got my attention."

My compassion told me to go slow. "That was just awful, but a large coincidence. We can't help but wonder if something was going on or if someone wanted to harm Slick or Lugnut."

Bianca gestured no. "They were both funny, warm men. I can't think of anyone who would want to hurt them."

Piper pressed. "Did Lugnut ever mention a secret mission in Vietnam? Linzi, his nurse, mentioned something about that."

Bianca chuckled. "She is a bit odd, that one. I would be cautious of anything she says. And Lugnut didn't ever mention anything like that." She turned to glance at Linzi. "I'm surprised she came tonight, she knows the family and I are not real fond of her."

The awkward silence that followed was broken by Piper. "So, do you still have Lugnut's heart pills?"

Bianca flipped her hands. "I guess. He had multiple bottles of them all over the house."

"Is there any way we can take a look at them?" My conscience immediately scolded me for being insensitive.

It must have showed, because Bianca responded with a smile. "It's alright, Ginger. I would expect you to be curious after the stories I have heard about you and your friends. Last summer the boys went to see a race, and

Dog stayed with us a couple of days. He told us all kind of stories and bragged about stakeouts and taking down bad guys."

Humility was not Piper's strong suit, but she surprised me. "I am sure he exaggerated. We mostly helped the police do their job."

Bianca continued. "Is it true your grumpy chicken ghost helps you sometimes?"

I snorted. "That is true. Although it's not always obvious that she is trying to help."

Bianca pointed. "They have a nice little spread put out for us over in another room. I could use a cup of coffee. Please join me. I have a bunch of questions for you, too.

Chapter Twelve

"So, what's with the heat?" Slick chuckled at his own question as he pointed at the hospital security personnel.

The VA police officer scowled at him and spoke with an annoyed tone. "I think you've seen one too many movies. We're vets, just like you, who simply keep the peace here. I would never go so far as to call us heat."

"I was just trying to keep things light." Slick's voice trailed off.

Dog said, "Look, Lugnut's heart attack followed by your accident is too big a coincidence. Something is going on."

Slick's eyebrows rose. "I'll say. And you forgot to tell me why you're in a wheelchair."

The nurse cut in and turned to Slick, "Did this happen to you right after using your oxygen?"

Candy responded. "It happened while using it. I found him with the mask still on, pulled down around his neck."

Slick nodded. "Yeah, I remember trying to pull it off when my head got real light."

Dog resumed. "Look, I think someone might have killed Lugnut. And they tried to kill you, too."

The nurse spoke to the officer, "He has been insisting

on this story and he was obsessed with talking to his friend here."

Slick scanned the various faces in the room. "Alright. You have some valid points. But you still haven't told me why you're in a wheelchair."

Dog sighed and blushed a little. "That's kind of embarrassing. I took a whiff of your oxygen, too."

Slick let out a belly laugh. "You think what happened to me is strange. But you're also in here because of my oxygen? That's so weird it's funny."

Dog mumbled. "I ran into a finicky cabbie and tried to show him the oxygen tank was harmless. But it wasn't."

"Okay, that's not weird, nooooooo. But I'll come back to this cabbie thing. The real question is, how did you get my oxygen tank?"

Dog hung his head a little. "I snuck through a window to take a look around your place."

Slick chuckled. "Okay, that's what I guessed. Now tell me, why did you feel the need to snoop around my place?"

Dog groaned leaned to one side of his wheelchair. "You won't believe me."

Slick's face became tight. "Try me."

"You remember Star? She runs a new age store next

to the pub and she sees and hears things. And sometimes she has dreams that come true. Star had a dream about Lugnut and saw his heart attack before it happened. Then Lugnut's ghost showed up in her shower and said I was in danger. Then you almost get killed." Dog closed his eyes and drooped his head. "I needed to take a look around for more clues as to what's going on."

Candy stared at Slick and went white. "So, all those weird Scooby-Doo stories you told me were true?"

The nurse held out her hand toward Dog, but spoke to the VA officer. "See why I wanted you here? This is all so bizarre."

The VA policeman stared at Dog Breath. "I thought you looked familiar. I saw you on that TV show, The Ghost Hounds."

The nurse huffed. "You know him?"

"Yeah. Him and his friends solved the murder of the show host. He was killed while filming an episode in The Grumpy Chicken Irish Pub."

The nurse gasped. "I do remember hearing something about that."

Candy started crying. "This is so scary. Someone tried to kill you!"

Dog cut her off. "Now, we don't know that. But it is why I wanted to look around your place, to see if there was anything that suggested foul play."

The sound carried through the hall and was easily heard in Slick's room. Dog Breath sat up straight and cleared his throat. "It looks like we going to have a few more visitors. I recognize that voice."

Everyone stared at Dog for a few seconds, until the doorway filled with the massive frame of a man. Guardrail spotted Dog first. "What are you doing in a wheelchair?"

Star and Edith trailed in behind Guardrail. The nurse studied each one as they came in. "We're going to need a bigger room."

Dog smiled at his friend. "This has been a long day and it's good to see you again."

Guardrail grinned. "Same here. Now what's going on. We came to see your old army buddy, and we thought you might be here, but what happened to you?"

Dog turned red and pinched his lips tight. Edith responded, "Looks like he did something stupid. That would be my guess."

The VA policeman scanned the new visitors and his face lit up, then he blurted out. "You're Guardrail, and you're Star!"

The nurse shook her head in disgust. "I asked for you to accompany us so you could help me with security. Not to get autographs of reality TV personalities. And why do you know these two?"

The VA officer gushed. "Guardrail is hard to forget.

And everyone remembers Star, she is psychic and so pretty. And she played in a band. Where is Ginger?"

Edith replied, "She had work to do elsewhere."

Dog finally picked his head up off his chest and spoke with a full voice. "I'm sorry guys. I couldn't let go of this thing that happened to Slick, especially after Lugnut. I had to look around his place to see if I could find something. I guess maybe I did. But it didn't work out so well."

Guardrail chuckled. "I guess not. I see a wrist bracelet and a wheelchair under you. How you got admitted here is mystery to me, but we thought you might come to visit Slick. So, we were kind of right."

Edith walked over to Dog's side. "Are you alright? With your unexpected departure from Dog's wake, we were worried about you, and from the looks of things our concerns were well founded."

Dog waved her comment off. "I'm fine. Thanks for worrying."

Star leaned against the wall. "Is there any chance I could get some water. I feel a little ill."

The nurse grabbed a water pitcher from a bedside table and a clean plastic cup. She poured some water and held it out to Star. "Are you alright? You look white? Here, let me look at you."

Star forced a small smile. "Trust me, it's not anything you have been trained for. I sense immense confusion and fear in this room. But I cannot discern who it is coming from. And there is another presence, an evil spirit, that I can't explain."

The nurse took a step back. "What are you some kind of witch?"

The police officer chuckled. "I told you she was psychic."

The nurse folded her arms and used a firm, official voice. "Alright, listen up. This has gone far enough for now. I am taking Mr. Bell back to his room."

Star crumpled her face. "Who is Mr. Bell?"

The nurse shrugged. "Alright, Dog Breath. What is with these ridiculous nick names. Really, you don't even know his real name?"

Dog held up his hand to stop her. "Not yet. There are a couple of things I need to take care of. Guardrail, I took Slick's oxygen tank and Lugnut's heart pills. The hospital is testing them and we should be able to learn if they contained poison, or something that would kill."

The nurse tilted her head back. "I almost forgot we were doing that."

Edith smiled. "Well, looks like you made some progress, Dog. But we will take it from here since it looks like you're out of commission for the time being."

Dog popped in his seat. "No! Don't leave me here alone. Lugnut's ghost said I was in danger, remember?"

Candy took Slick's hand and fussed. "I'm staying here with you, baby. I'm not letting you out of my sight."

Slick smiled back at her. "You are too good to me."

Guardrail glanced at the two love birds, then looked to Edith. "Can you stay with Dog?"

Edith held up her bag. "Sure. I got my knitting right here and can use some quiet time."

Guardrail stepped over to Star and touched her hand. "Are you going to be alright? Do you need an aspirin? I'm willing to bet a hospital might be a good place to get a couple if you do. Although they may cost $30 bucks each."

Star grinned at him. "No, but that is sweet of you. So, what are we going to do next?"

Guardrail's face became taunt. "We need to head back to the funeral home. Dog did a good job getting the heart medicine and gas to testing. But it made me think. If someone messed with Lugnut's pills, they might be able to find traces of the poison in the body. We need to go back to the funeral home and talk with them. And we need to contact the state mortician."

The VA policeman cut in. "I can help with that. I might know someone to call who works with the state morgue."

Star added. "Guardrail, we should call someone, too. Ginger and Piper are at the funeral home. They can talk to whoever runs the funeral home and ask them to isolate Lugnut's body. So, then the question is still, what do we do next?"

Guardrail shrugged. "I guess we accompany Dog back to his room and call Ginger. We can compare notes with the gang at Lugnut's wake. If anyone could learn something from the people at the wake, it's Piper and Ginger. And with the test results from the pills and gas tank Dog found, maybe we will know where to go from there."

The policeman glanced to the nurse. "Looks like we need to light a fire under the lab. We have a crime to solve."

The nurse snickered. "We? So, you're a member of this?"

"No. Both of us are. Something is going on and we can help make sure no one else gets hurt. It's the right thing to do."

"Thank you, officer. There is danger and you are right. There is an evil presence that surrounds all of these events. We need to stop whoever is doing this before they hurt someone else." Star's voice showed genuine concern.

Chapter Thirteen

My phone vibrated as I nibbled on a chicken salad slider. Some mayo had oozed out onto my hands, and I wiped them clean on my jeans so I could take out my cell. "Hello?"

"Ginger, it's Guardrail. We're at the hospital and we found Dog. But you aren't going to believe this, he was admitted as a patient."

My mind froze. "Is he alright?"

"Yeah, I can tell he is alright because he's ornery as ever."

The surprises just kept coming and I felt my mental balance was off, like I was leaning back too far in a chair and was almost at the tipping point. "What happened?"

"To be honest, I'm not one hundred percent sure. But he's not going anywhere. Edith is going to stay with him, make sure he is alright. But then what should Star and me do?"

"That's a good question. As it happens, there is one thing I was told here at the wake that keeps bothering me. A nurse here told me that Dog and his friends may have been involved in some sort of top-secret mission while over in Vietnam."

Guardrail's laughter was so loud it hurt me ear. It took

him a few seconds to settle down and say, "Dog? Really, he is the last man I would want to handle a top-secret mission in wartime."

"Yeah, I thought so, too. But then I remembered they were younger back then, and maybe they were perfect for something like that working out of the motor pool. You know, not on the front lines but there and free to spy, or whatever. And Dog did say there were times that when he was out with Lugnut he thought they might die. I always thought that statement was odd, but if they were spying or doing something covert…"

"I hate when you make sense only to complicate things. How the heck are we going to look into something like that?" Guardrail let out a big sigh. "I can ask Dog, I guess, since we are here with him."

"Exactly what I was thinking. And how about his friend, Slick?" You can ask him, too."

"His wife, or girlfriend, or whoever she was, I don't know. We were never really introduced, but there is another woman in the room. And they were acting like love struck teenagers. Talking to Slick might be more difficult."

The huff of air I released was amplified by the receiver. "You can ask her to leave. Let her know you need to talk in private in order to follow up on all that has happened recently."

Guardrail groaned. "I guess. I just don't like being so forward."

"Wait a minute. You don't have to. Send Edith back to Slick's room to question him. She has no problem getting to the point, even if it ruffles a few feathers. Just send her."

"Bingo, and Star and I will try to get the test results while she does."

"Great! Wait, what test results?"

Guardrail chuckled. "Dog somehow managed to get Lugnut's heart pills *and* Slick's oxygen. The hospital is testing them right now."

"The bombshells keep on coming, don't they? At least Dog left you guys hanging at the wake for a good reason. Alright, tell Edith to call us with whatever she learns from Slick. When you get all that test info, Grab Star and head back to Lugnut's wake and meet up with us here. There are a couple of other loose ends we need to pin down, but we can address those when you get here."

"Will do." Guardrail must have been motivated because he hung up with even saying goodbye.

I turned to Piper. "This day has been so weird, so if I told you Dog was admitted to the hospital, would you be surprised?"

"Nope. He should have been admitted years ago." Piper smiled at me but I could tell she was a little shocked. "So, what happened?"

"Guardrail didn't really know, but he's going to meet

us here in a bit. So, we will find out more then. And you probably heard, I asked him to ask both Dog and Slick about that odd comment from Linzi. You know, the top-secret thing?"

"We think alike. I kept going back to that. But Dog doesn't seem like the spy type."

"Yeah, but that is now. He was a lot younger back then, and probably a different man."

Piper raised an eyebrow. "I didn't think of that. So, you're thinking it makes sense to check it out just in case."

"Yeah. And with everything that has happened, the unexpected seems to be the path we're on."

Bianca took up a conversation with a well-dressed, older woman when I took the phone call. But now that I was off, she attempted to resume our conversation before I could tell Piper about the tests that were being run. Bianca asked, "You were asking if I got along with Linzi?"

The words failed to come to me, but Piper jumped in. "Yes, you know, was it awkward with her being so close to Lugnut as his nurse?"

Bianca chuckled. "Lugnut was married once before me, and he had a few girlfriends. I knew that going in. And Lugnut was my third husband, we were not exactly a young doe eyed couple. So, a nurse showing him some extra attention was not a big deal in my book."

Piper continued. "So, why was Lugnut Linzi's favorite patient?"

"It's kind of complicated. The fact Lugnut was married did not bother Linzi. She liked him, a lot, so she pursued him even if he was married. She even asked me if I was happy in our marriage. But she figured out pretty quick it was not going to happen. However, it did almost come between Slick and Lugnut because Slick had a thing for Linzi for a while. But she wasn't interested in Slick and he eventually moved on to Candy."

I asked, "Did Linzi take being rejected by Lugnut poorly?"

Bianca paused, then answered. "Linzi didn't take being rejected by Lugnut that bad. Just after it happened, she was kind of cold for a while when we went for checkups and things at the hospital, but eventually she got over it."

Piper asked before I could. "How did you know Slick liked Linzi?"

Bianca chuckled. "Slick likes the ladies. And he wasn't shy about talking about it. He must have said a thousand times while he and Lugnut were hanging out and drinking beers 'I'm gonna make her my lady.' Or something like that."

Piper rubbed her temples. "I feel like I'm in high school again. That is like every conversation I had at lunch in the tenth grade."

Bianca smiled politely at Piper. "You have to understand the military. These boys are special for what they sacrificed and risked. But you're right, they like to have a good time and can be a bit juvenile at times. Who's got a bigger truck? Who can spit further? It's all about competition and being the best. And Linzi likes being around it so she did provoke them a little. But like I said, Lugnut was never interested in her and Slick's interest faded away when he found Candy. But Linzi still took good care of both of them, even coming out to the houses to help at times."

I could see Bianca was trying to be nice, but she was tiring of the conversation. "We are just trying to figure out who might want to hurt Slick or Lugnut. And lover quarrels are always of interest. Sorry we asked so many questions."

"It's okay, Ginger. I understand. But for a lover's quarrel, you're better off speaking to Candy, Slick's girlfriend. She and Linzi are like oil and water."

"Thanks Bianca, for all the information and talking with us. This is a hard day for you and we appreciate you taking the time." I reached out to shake her hand.

"You're more than welcome. And I asked you more questions than you asked me. I can't believe I talked your ear off about that pub of yours. I'm sure Lugnut is up there watching all this and he was thrilled to have you all here. He loved all of Dog's stories and always watched the episode about the pub whenever it was rerun. He must have watched it twenty times." Bianca reached out and hugged me. "We don't shake hands around here, we hug."

Piper giggled but followed suit and joined the hug. "Thank you from me, too. And we're sorry for your loss."

"What's going on here? Looks like a group hug. I see you ladies have made friends fast." Digger had a stupid look on his face.

Piper snapped back. "You jealous we can make friends and you can't?"

"Au contraire, my pretty journalist friend. I made a good buddy and he told me a thing or two that was really interesting." Digger folded his arms to show his confidence.

Dixie bounded up next to him. "Why did you take off so fast. I had that old soldier telling us his life story?

Piper squinted at Digger. "You made a good buddy?"

"Well, I was there! So, maybe it was more like Dixie and me." Digger looked at his toes as his voice trailed off.

Dixie glanced back at the man they'd been talking to. "According to these guys, it seems that Lugnut and Slick were quite the duo at the VA. Everybody knew them and this nurse named Linzi. Seems the three of them were the life of the party."

Piper let out a low indiscernible grumble. "So, if they were so popular, who would want to hurt both of them then? It makes no sense."

I added. "Guardrail will be here with Star in a little bit. Maybe we can put our heads together with what they learned and see if we can piece it together."

Bianca lit up. "Ginger, did you say Star was coming back? She said she might try to talk to Lugnut's spirit for me."

I nodded yes. "They should be here in a little bit. They were at the VA hospital and had a couple of things to do first, but then they were going to leave right after that."

Bianca went and found the well-dressed woman she was talking to earlier. She said something in her ear and they both picked their heads up and giggled.

When Bianca was out of earshot, Piper spoke with a soft voice. "There's an awful lot of love here in Statesboro. Too much if you ask me. This nurse going after a married man, Slick chasing multiple woman. And everyone seems amused by it all. Except Lugnut is dead, albeit maybe of natural causes. But then Slick is put in the hospital. My woman's intuition is telling me some of the nooky went spooky."

Dixie cocked her head to one side. "Did Piper just make a pun? Well, paint me green and call me a pickle. It wasn't all that great, but not bad for a journalist."

Piper glared at Dixie and shot back. "I don't need to paint you any color to call you names. Watch it!" Then she smiled at the tough bartender and shrugged. We all allowed ourselves a short laugh, after which, we decided to check out the buffet to eat finger food and drink coffee as we waited for Star and Guardrail.

Chapter Fourteen

Star and Guardrail made good time and met us at the funeral home. The big guy was hungry and helped himself to the buffet. Star, on the other hand, didn't touch a thing. She looked tired and she grabbed a cup of coffee.

Guardrail pinched his eyebrows and shrugged. "I'm telling ya, there was nothing wrong with Lugnut's heart pills. They checked multiple pills and they didn't find anything wrong with them. To do more detailed testing they need more time, but the lab tech was pretty sure the pills are normal."

Piper sighed. "Well, maybe he died of natural causes then."

Star jumped in. "No, something happened to him. I can feel it. And all the pieces fit. The test results do surprise me, but that doesn't prove it wasn't foul play. We need to test his body."

I rolled my eyes. "Who is going to ask the grieving widow?"

Digger cleared his throat. "Well, we don't have to. Can't we get the police to do that?"

Piper replied, "I suppose, but that will take forever."

Dixie cut in, "Hey, if the hospital could test the pills, couldn't they test his body?"

I whined and pointed across the hall to the room where the wake was being held. "The body is in the coffin. They are ready to bury him."

Dixie continued, "Yeah, but this is kind of an emergency, or at least a special case. Right?"

Guardrail cleared his throat in a cocksure manner. "Are you all through here? I got it covered."

Star nudged him. "We have it covered!"

The big man smiled back at her and continued. "Alright, we have it covered. The VA policeman we met is calling the local morgue. He is going to let me know, but he was pretty sure they would follow up on it and test Lugnut after what happened to Slick."

"Alright, so we have a potential way to test the body. But we still don't have a person-of-interest list." I pinched my lips when done out of frustration.

"I know what you mean, Ginger. My current person-of-interest list all have strong ties to the VA hospital, but we know little about other friends and family." Piper shook her head to emphasize the point.

Digger bounced from me to Piper with his eyes. "You have people of interest already?"

Piper shrugged. "Yeah, that nurse was a bit off, what was her name? Linzi, that's right. And we have Slick's girlfriend who doesn't get along with the nurse. And the nurse tried to steal Bianca's husband. Any of those three ladies had some motive."

Digger shook his head no. "I think the government is covering something up. That makes more sense. And they're cleaning up things by getting rid of these guys."

Piper moaned and threw her head back. "Really, Digger? The Vietnam war was over forty years ago. You honestly think the government is just getting around to covering up what they did back then now? I don't think so. And Dog and his friends don't strike me as the spy type."

Guardrail waved his hands in the air. "Can we get back to the test results? We're getting side tracked."

I pinched my eyebrows and wrinkled my nose. "Why? The tests came up empty."

"The pills did. But not the oxygen tank. In fact, the Army guys were very concerned that the tank had a top-secret gas in it. The VA police confiscated it and were very clear that we needed to turn over anything else that might have the gas, too. You could see there was a sense of urgency and concern."

Dixie sucked in a short burst of air and blurted out. "Is anyone else adding this up. A top-secret gas and a weird story about a top-secret mission? Maybe it is not as out there as we thought?"

Digger's eyes grew. "See, I told you it was a possibility. And those government agents don't fool around to keep things secret."

Guardrail huffed. "The gas is weird, yes. But I have

known Dog for many years, like a brother. And there is very little I don't know about him. He is no spy. But I've been thinking about the odd gas in Slick's tank. Maybe Lugnut was not the target? Maybe it was Slick?"

Piper snorted out her nose. "You know, Guardrail, that is pretty insightful. From the start I have been cautious about Lugnut's heart attack. It could have been just that, and nothing more. From the start, we've assumed it was more because of Star's experiences. However, Lugnut's ghost saying Dog was in danger could mean a lot of things. It doesn't have to mean that Lugnut was murdered."

"To be honest, I've had the same thought, Piper. But everyone does say Lugnut was in good health and the heart attack surprised people, so maybe it was caused by something in his pills. Heart attacks do happen suddenly sometimes." I moved my hands like they were a balance scale trying to figure out which side was heavier.

Dixie added, "But Star also saw a woman in her dream giving something to Lugnut. So, that tells us two things. It was a woman who did it and someone did poison Lugnut, if her dream is right."

Piper forced a smile and made eye contact with Star. "It was a dream. With all due respect, it doesn't mean that is what really happened."

Star seemed to be lost in thought for a moment, then replied. "I know it is hard for others to understand. But there are things I see in dreams that are real, and I know it actually happened or is going to happen. There is no doubt about that dream being an actual event."

"Are you alright, Star? You sound so tired?" Dixie had compassion in her voice, the real kind and not the forced version she used when tending bar.

Star formed a faint smile. "Yeah, I'm fine. I'm tired for sure. The dream and the build up to the encounter with Lugnut's spirit was draining and I have not slept much since. And I know this is weird, but I have felt an evil presence the whole time we have been in Statesboro. It was in Slick's hospital room and at the wake earlier today, but it was faint. But I am feeling it again, right now, and it is really strong. I can feel it sapping my energy."

Digger surprised us all when he patted Star on the shoulder and said, "We got your back. Is there anything I can do for ya? You want an aspirin or something?"

Star chuckled. "Why do you and Guardrail think an aspirin can help with paranormal issues?"

Digger's face went blank. "I guess I just assumed the weird ghost stuff gave you a headache."

Star shook her head no. "An aspirin is not going to fix this. We have to find this evil entity and defeat it, that's the only thing that will lift this crushing weight I'm feeling."

Piper eyed Star wearily. "So, if we assume it is a

woman based on Star's dream, I have three, Bianca, Candy, and Linzi. They have had run ins with one another, and they all had good access to both Slick and Lugnut."

Digger uttered. "Don't forget the government cover up angle! That could explain the secret gas."

I could not keep the thought to myself, so I added, "So, I think we are back to testing Lugnut's body. Regardless of whether it was a male or female, if it was some kind of poison or medication that caused his heart attack, testing his remains is the best way to confirm it. And to get others, like the police, to believe this story."

Dixie burst into laughter. "I would love to see a police detective's face if we told him this story."

Guardrail didn't laugh, and even looked pensive. Then he said, "Ginger, the VA policeman is helping us. And he knows the local police and he can inform them if we find anything. Plus, he believes in the Grumpy Chicken ghost. He loved the TV appearance and knew us from it."

"How much did you tell him? Have you told him the whole story already?" I scolded myself internally for worrying about getting the police involved. But a part of me felt it was too soon. We needed some actual evidence before we involved them.

"He knows pretty much everything. He was in the room when Dog and Slick talked, and they covered just about everything." Guardrail looked up and to the right, like he was rewinding and replaying a tape of the event.

My phone rang and vibrated, and I answered. "Hello?"

"Ginger, it's Dad. We had an unusual incident here you might want to know about."

"Um, how unusual."

Dad chuckled. "Not very for this place. But you know that old white board we have in the back?"

"Yeah."

"Well, something appeared on it. It's a few letters that are kind of hard to read because they are like a watery lens floating around on the whiteboard. And you can see right through the letters like you're looking into the center of the universe."

"Well, that is different. Could you make out what letters are floating around on the board?"

Dad sniffled. "Kind of. I think Bones is more confident about it than I am. Let me put him on the phone."

There was some rustling then Bones' voice blared from the earpiece. "Ginger? You there?"

"Yep. Dad said you might have made out the letters on the board. Do you know what letters are there?"

"Yeah. It was hard because they move and are kind of like liquid. And they pass through each other as they move. It's kind of creepy, but you can see these beautiful stars through them."

"I get it. We're talking about the Grumpy Chicken here and these things happen. Now can you tell me what letters are floating around on the board?"

"Yeah. There are two, C's, A's, R's and O's, and there is one M and Z."

"Wait, I have to write this down. Anyone got a pen and paper?" I held my hand out and waited.

Piper jumped and produced the little notebook and pen she always kept with her in case she ran into a story.

I continued. "Okay, two each of C, A, R, and O, and only of M and Z. Is that right?"

Bones mumbled to himself then responded. "Yeah, that is what I think is there. I took a video of it with my phone. I can send it to you."

I hung my head and looked at my scribbles on the note page. "I can't believe I didn't think of that. But, yeah, please send the video so we can see it. And thanks for calling."

Bones let out a nervous laugh. "How are you doing up there? You figure this all out yet?"

"No, but thanks for calling and tell Dad I will call later tonight. I need to go now. Bye."

I clicked the phone off and put it in my pocket. Not

surprisingly, the gang had watched closely and they'd heard the whole phone call.

Piper quipped, "Well?"

I snorted and looked at the letters on the piece of paper. "Anyone up for a game of scrabble?"

The puzzled looks I got in reply were expected. But then I saw their jaws drop and eyes pop. It was clear something even stranger than the phone call had happened behind me, so I spun to look. I saw two military MP's marching into the funeral home accompanied by two other somber looking men. It was obvious none of the four were happy to be here and they headed straight into the room where Lugnut's wake was taking place.

Chapter Fifteen

"Piper, see what they're here for. I'm assuming they came to get samples from Lugnut's body." My mind was racing and I needed to get organized to make sure we didn't miss anything.

Dixie joked, "What do you think they have to do, take out a whole organ, like a liver or something?"

Digger turned white. "I hate the thought of that."

Dixie couldn't contain her laugh. "A grave digger that can't take a little blood?"

"Nope, I work with the dirt, not the bodies."

Star peeked around the corner from the small cafe area where we had settled. "They are talking to Bianca and Piper is there, too. Has to be they want to get some test specimens."

"I think you're right, Star, but we can't assume. So, we should wait for Piper to come back tell us what was going on. So what do we do while we wait? We have this Grumpy Chicken letter thing to figure out and we still need to check out Slick and Lugnut's background, as well as their wives and girlfriends."

"Ginger, I think the gas is an important piece, too. If it was top secret, who had access and how did they get it? That may answer a lot of questions." Dixie's voice wavered a little, like she was unsure if she should say what she was thinking. It wasn't like her to sound indecisive.

"I agree, but it might be hard to find out about the gas with the military guys cracking down. But we do have one ace in the hole. Slick is alive and Dog and Edith are there with him. And I think we need to learn more about Slick's girlfriend, Candy, and it's time to ask Slick some pointed questions, like who had clearance to get near a gas like the one that almost killed him. And who would want to kill him."

Digger had been fidgeting and stopped to contribute a thought. "We should talk to Lugnut, too."

Guardrail glared down at the old grave digger. "Have you lost your mind? The man is dead."

"No, I think I know what he is thinking." I smiled at Digger as a thanks.

Star smiled at me. "Ginger, you have more ability to sense than you give yourself credit for. You can feel the evil presence, too. I can tell. And you know that Bianca asked me to try and contact Lugnut."

Digger assumed a smug face. "See Guardrail? I have good ideas, too. Star can talk to Lugnut."

"I'm not sure I would ever call talking to a ghost a good idea." Guardrail shivered as he finished.

Star continued. "I agree we should try to make contact. But I'm not sure it would be the right time with all that is going on. Maybe I can plan to do a private session with Bianca first thing in the morning. It is getting late tonight and I'm guessing she will not be all that keen to do it late tonight after the MP's crashed the party."

I nodded in agreement. "It will also give us time to call Dog and Edith at the VA hospital and coordinate all the questions we want to ask, and to who."

Digger smirked. "We need to ask both Lugnut and Slick about any funny stuff they might have done over in Vietnam."

"Yeah, I know. But I also want to know more about this little dating game they were playing at the VA, too. Poison and gas are an odd choice to kill someone, and that feels like a woman's touch." Thinking out loud was becoming my standard procedure.

Guardrail sighed. "So, that means we're not even sure who the intended target is. Slick or Lugnut, but it feels more like Slick given the unusual gas used in his oxygen tank."

Digger rubbed his eyes. "This is getting too complicated, it's hurting my brain."

Guardrail added, "We asked Slick already who may want to hurt him, but maybe we need to press a little harder."

"We need to get Ida's help. She needs to fire up her computers and those little web crawlers to do some background checking for us. I think she should do it tonight. The sooner the better."

"That's a good idea, Ginger. I feel we're still missing something." Star's eyes drifted off to inspect the scene back in the wake once more.

"Well, while we're waiting let's see those letters. I am good at the daily jumble." Digger rubbed his hands together like he was going to crack a safe.

Dixie snorted, "You? Your vocabulary consists of six words."

Digger glared at the snarky bartender and then held his hand out. I gave him the notepad with the letters. He scribbled a bit and then stopped, staring at the notes like he had just painted a masterpiece. "There ya go! It spells 'orzo masccara.'"

Dixie laughed and tapped his notes. "I'm pretty sure mascara is spelled with only one C. And what in Asgard is orzo mascara?"

Digger rubbed his chin. "You sure it only has one C? And what in the blue hills is Asgard?"

Guardrail did not look at him but replied. "You know, the planet that Thor and Loki come from."

Digger shook his head. "Thor? Really? And you all think orzo mascara is weird."

Piper came shooting back into the dining area. "They are doing it right here, right now!"

Digger turned white again. "I think I need to go outside and get some fresh air."

Piper scowled at him. "Suck it up, will ya. They're just taking some hair and tissue samples. It's not big deal."

"Did they tell you when they would have results?"

"Yeah, Ginger, they did. Tomorrow." Piper pinched her lips and raised her eyebrows in an attempt to non verbally brag about her journalist skills.

Guardrail brought her back to earth. "Well, they going to share them with us?"

Piper shrugged. "Don't know. They said maybe, but we have to tell them everything we know first. Then they may share the results with us."

"Well, we don't really know all the much. And a good deal of it deals with Star's insights. I'm not sure how much faith those military men will have in the mystic side of things."

Star chuckled. "Ginger, as always you are right. Those men strike me as the kind who would doubt it."

Digger sighed. "Well, it's always best to tell the truth. Always! That was what my momma said."

Dixie rolled her eyes. "Here we go. Whenever you mention your momma, you're covering up for something."

Digger frowned. "I just don't want to be the one who tells government employed MP's that the government is causing all this. You know, since I'm the only one who thinks it is a government cover up."

Piper continued. "The MP's told me that Guardrail and Star are to communicate with the VA policeman they met earlier. He's keeping an eye on Slick and Dog for now and we can talk to him. He is our point of contact, and he will relay the information up the chain."

"That sounds like a one-way street." My lips pinched together in frustration.

Guardrail noticed. "Maybe not, Ginger. I talked to this guy and I think he would love to be involved on one of our adventures. I could hear it in his voice and see it in his eyes. He will tell us all that he can, I'm sure of it."

Star nodded. "I agree. I sensed excitement in him, the kind you see in a child going to Disney World."

"It's still a big leap of faith. And I suspect we'll really want to know the results of those tests they're running tonight." I glanced to Piper for other ideas.

"I think you're right, Ginger. But what other choice do we have? For now, we can try and solve the letters thing and get some sleep. It is going to be a long day tomorrow." Piper wrinkled her forehead as she searched for more.

Digger interrupted. "I solved the letter thing. It spells orzo mascara." He held the note page out for Piper to see.

Piper sighed. "Digger, I don't want to hurt your feelings, but mascara is spelled with only one C."

Dixie could not keep quiet. "See I told ya. Keep trying."

Star piped up. "I need to talk to Bianca. We might be able to do a séance tomorrow to talk to Lugnut. She wanted to try, and if connect with him, we can ask some questions about what happened to him."

"So, you need us to go with you to talk with Bianca?"

"Thanks, Ginger, it would be appreciated. I am exhausted and I'm sure I could use some help with the courtesies."

Piper threw out, "I'll go, too. Let's go get it done. I'm sure she'll say yes."

So Star, Piper and I left Guardrail and Digger with the food and coffee to go schedule a séance.

Chapter Sixteen

We returned to the hotel and assembled in the bar. We were full from all the nibbling at the wake, but grabbed a nightcap and corner table to chat about our day. "I guess it's time to call Ida."

Piper nodded in agreement. "We could use a break, and she felt left out. I can call if you want."

"No, I'll call." I took out my phone and dialed.

"Hey, Ginger. How's it going?" Ida sounded chipper.

"Well, we could use some help. Things are kind of complicated here and we need to see if you can find something of interest for a few people."

"Will do! Send me the names and any other info you think may help me."

"Thanks. You sound awful cheerful. Anything happen back there in Potter's Mill we should know about?"

"Not really. I heard from Scooter today, that's all. He called from Scotland. They're shooting in some old castle over there."

I chuckled. "I should have guessed. Well, I'm glad you're in a good mood. You might be up late with this one, because we need to get some results from you by early tomorrow morning."

"No problem." Ida talked while she chewed something.

Piper cut in. "I just sent all the names to Ida's phone. Tell her to call us if she needs anything else."

"Ida…"

"I heard, Piper's voice carries. I'll get right on it. Talk to you in the morning. I need to get going to get this done, talk to you later." Ida clicked off.

"Well, that's done." I put my phone back into my pocket.

Guardrail asked, "You got those jumbled letters. I want to play with them, see if I can come up with something better than orzo mascara."

Digger blushed. "At least I tried."

Piper took command. "Here, I can put each letter on a separate piece of paper, that we can move around to see if we can see if it spells anything."

Star added. "A "Z" doesn't get used very much, so I thought when I first saw it that the Z might make it easier."

"I thought the same thing." Piper ripped out a few sheets from her small wire bound note book and wrote a Z on one of them. "There's the Z." Then she wrote all the other letters on their own piece.

Guardrail fussed with a few of the letters. "There, no

that makes no sense."

Star wondered, "I think the Z may be used in the word razor?"

Piper shuffled the letters around. "So that leaves M, A, S, and two C's. I'm not sure you can spell anything with that."

Digger sat up straight. "Casm…no." Digger slumped back in his chair.

Piper added, "Maybe the Z is not for the word razor."

"Wait a minute." I took out my phone and did a quick internet search. "The word finder apps give me comas, but we still have an extra C."

Star sighed, "If the Z is not used in razor, what other words could use the Z?"

Piper popped. "No, maybe we're missing punctuation. I had a college professor that always said sometimes the facts point to a strange conclusion. And our minds don't like unexpected or unusual answers. So, we tend to ignore the most obvious conclusion as determined by the facts. But when you have competing theories to explain something, you should go with the theory that has the least assumptions. In other words, the simplest answer is usually the right one, no matter how unexpected it may be. There was a name for this philosophy for solving problems, Occam's razor. If you add an apostrophe, the letters spell Occam's razor."

Digger scrunched up his face. "Well, that makes no

sense. Why would the Grumpy Chicken want to tell us Occam's razor?"

"She is telling us to keep it simple. Follow the facts." I tapped Occam's razor into my phone's browser and read the search results. "Seems our spectral chicken is pretty smart. But, why is she telling us to keep it simple and use the answer with the fewest assumptions?"

Piper snorted. "That makes some sense. We don't know if Lugnut was poisoned yet. We don't know how someone could get a hold of a top-secret gas. We don't know of anyone who would have a motive to kill anyone. That all means we have to make assumptions, and that has bothered me since we started on this."

I shrugged. "So, we have to follow what the evidence tells us, even it seems bizarre."

"Isn't that what I just said." Piper used her best snarky voice.

Star ignored our exchange. "I think that message from the chicken means something to me. I have sensed an evil entity here in Statesboro. And it makes sense if there is someone trying to kill others running around. But it is more than that and I have been trying to ignore it. If I am honest, and trust everything I have learned about the other side, I would have to say there is another medium here in Statesboro using her talents for no good."

Digger blinked a number of times. "What do you mean? There is someone else like you here that is the murderer?"

Star studied the old grave digger's crusty face. "Exactly. I didn't believe it, but the pieces all fit. Including Lugnut's spirit presenting itself to me so soon after his death. I think it is even more important to contact Lugnut's spirit tomorrow morning and try to find out who is using their spiritual talents for evil."

Guardrail let out a big burst of air. "Well, I'm not sure I can sleep after all this talk about ghosts, and using the other side for evil. But I think we should try to get some sleep. It is late and we have a loooong day in front of us tomorrow. I'm hitting the sack, goodnight."

"Guardrail is right, we should all get some sleep."

Chapter Seventeen

Bianca and Star agreed it would be better to hold the séance at the hotel and I made arrangements to use one of their meeting rooms. Star woke early and went to the room, making preparations for the séance. She rearranged the room so that she was comfortable. But she was missing the big crystal ball used for seances back in her new age shop.

To adapt, she placed a small lamp in the center of the conference table. She didn't plug it in and hoped it would work in the same manner as her prized crystal glove, glowing once for yes and twice for no to answer her questions. She removed the shade to expose the bulb as a stand in for a crystal ball.

Bianca was excited to conduct the séance and showed up early. "Good morning, Star. Are we ready to do this?"

Star pointed to a chair. "Yes, and it would work best if you sit here. All we need now is Piper and Dixie."

"I'll go get them." I hurried from the meeting room and headed upstairs. Piper and I shared a room and I knew she was still asleep when I left. I hoped she was up now.

As I entered the room, I heard the shower running. "Come on, Piper. You're holding us up! Bianca is here and Star is ready. She needs us down there, now!"

The shower water stopped and after a minute she emerged wearing a robe, her hair wrapped in a towel. "Son of a gun! I feel like I have a lead weight strapped onto my back today. And my head is buzzing, but I'll get it together."

There was a knock on the door and I answered. It was Dixie. "Come on guys, I went to the room and they said you came up to get Piper."

"Come on in Dixie. Now at least I don't have to go and track you down, too." I eyed Piper as I spoke to let her know she needed to pick things up.

After a few minutes she was dressed and she made one last stop in the bathroom to do her hair. I groaned. "Just brush it out and don't worry about it."

Piper surprisingly did just that, no fussing or blow drying. It was not like her, but we were in a hurry.

We headed for the elevator and went back downstairs to the meeting room. Star was waiting for us and smiled as we entered. "Perfect! We are all here now, so we can start. Piper can you turn the lights down?"

Piper complied, then we all took a seat. Star began, "Now, if we could all hold hands and form a circle."

We joined hands and Star closed her eyes. "Are there any benevolent spirits here that would like to communicate?" Star stared at the bare bulb of the small table lame. It did nothing.

Star repeated, "Are there any benevolent spirits here

that would like to communicate?"

The bulb did not even flicker. But there was a light, only it came from the charm hanging on a chain around Bianca's neck.

Star cocked her head and studied the glowing jewelry. "We have a spirit with us. And I think it is someone who loved Bianca." The charm glowed once again, one short pulse.

Bianca was shaking. "I'm scared. Am I going to be alright? I don't like this. Why is it messing with my jewelry?"

Star smiled. "Is the spirit with us the man they called Lugnut?"

The gondola shaped charm glowed once. Bianca broke into tears. "I am so stupid. Lugnut bought this necklace for me on our trip to Venice. It was my favorite trip ever, and I wear this necklace all the time."

Star grinned. "Lugnut loves you very much and he is trying to answer our questions, but he also wanted to let you know he loves you."

"I love you, too, you screwy old nut." Bianca wept and could hardly speak.

Star continued. "Lugnut, did someone tamper with your heart pills, causing your death?"

There was a pause, then suddenly the bare light bulb exploded sending glass shards flying. The five of us let go of each other's hands and covered our faces while ducking behind the table.

I sat back up and looked to Star. "Was that a yes?"

"I think so." Star checked herself for injuries as she answered.

Bianca sobbed. "My poor baby. Who would do this to you?"

Star looked around to make sure no one was hurt, and when she was sure we were all fine, she said, "Please rejoin hands. And we can only ask questions with a yes or no answer. I think it is best if I ask the questions."

The group clasped hands again and we all stared at Star. "Thank you Lugnut for coming and answering our questions. I know this is difficult for you. Did you know the person who did this to you?"

Bianca's necklace glowed bright once. Her tears were slightly subsiding and she pleaded with her eyes to Star.

Star understood. "Lugnut, are you at peace now?"

Bianca's necklace glowed with bright, white light, once.

Bianca blurted out. "That makes me feel so much better. Thank you, honey. I miss you so much already."

Dixie was white. She had been through one séance, but she didn't like it and that dislike was evident in her face now. She blurted out, "Come on Star, ask about the gas, too?"

Bianca pinched her eyebrows and frowned as she stared at Dixie. "What gas?"

Star intervened. "Bianca, we have questions for Lugnut, too. I'm so sorry for Dixie's outburst, but we do need to ask a few questions."

Bianca nodded. "I understand. The things that have happened the last few days are so strange. And we need to figure out who caused all this."

Star smiled at Bianca. "Thank you for understanding. I know finding out the truth about Lugnut's heart attack was hard. You are very strong and considerate to help us, Bianca."

"I want to help find who hurt the love of my life." Bianca had a slight growl when she said the word 'who.'

Star closed her eyes once again. "Lugnut, are you aware your friend Slick was hurt?" One flash. "Do you know how he was hurt?" One flash. "Do you know who did it to him?" One dim red flash.

Bianca almost swore, but she stopped herself then said, "This is so frustrating he can't tell us a name."

Star nodded, "I know, but let me ask a few more questions."

Bianca wiped her nose then nodded yes.

Star continued, "Is the person who did this to Slick still in Statesboro." One white flash. "Is it the same person who hurt you?" One white flash. "Did they hurt you both because of money?" Two white flashes. "The gas used to harm Slick is a military secret, do you know who would have access to a gas like that?" One white flash. "Is this person in the military?" Two white flashes. "Is the person male?" Two quick flashes.

Piper cleared her throat and shook her head. "Star, my head is buzzing and I feel like something is wrong."

"I noticed how quiet you were, Piper. I feel it, too." My head felt like ten swarms of bees were buzzing inside.

Star opened her eyes. "I have felt something since we started, but it is getting stronger. Lugnut, are you aware of an evil entity that is working against us?" One white flash. "Is the entity on the other side with you?"

Nothing. Dixie whined, "That is not helpful."

Star wrinkled her forehead. "Is this entity with us?" Nothing. "The entity must be on your side or ours. Are you still here with us, Lugnut? One flash. "Then I am confused, it must…wait, is there a medium working with an evil spirit on your side? One flash. "So, the evil is operating on both sides." A single flash again. Star pinched her eyebrows. "Are we safe, now, here in the hotel?" Nothing. "Have these evil entities completed their work?" Two bright red flashes from the necklace.

Chapter Eighteen

Guardrail made the turn into Dog's hospital room. "What are you doing out of bed? And why are you out of your hospital gown?"

"I'm going home. Well, at least I'm being discharged this morning."

Edith was curled up in a chair in the corner, still asleep. Dog got an awful grin and tip toed over to her. He picked up a loose strand of yarn from her knitting and held so it dangled a few inches from his hand. Then he hung over Edith's face lowered it till it just touched her nose, tickling it ever slow slightly.

Without warning she picked up one of the knitting needles and wielded it like a knife, barely missing Dog's thigh.

Guardrail broke into laughter. "Careful there, Dog. You almost became a patient again."

Dog glared at Edith. "I was just fooling with ya. And who knew you had the reflexes of a cat?"

Edith picked up her knitting supplies and said, "You're lucky they aren't as good as they used to be, or you would have a knitting needle sticking out of your leg right now."

Dog shot a glance to Guardrail to see if he thought the old spinster was joking. But Guardrail raised an eyebrow and frowned.

Dog grunted. "Dang. Well, I learn something new every day."

"What's going on in here? I see we have a party already." The VA policeman smiled at Guardrail, but then studied Digger. "Who's he?"

Guardrail glanced to Digger and then back to the policeman. "He is another of our friends from Potter's Mill. His name is Digger."

"Nice to meet you. They call me Heat." The VA policeman grinned after announcing his new nickname.

Edith waved at him and whined. "Oh, just because Slick called you Heat, and Candy liked it, doesn't make it a nickname."

"True. But all the nurses and other VA blues liked it, too. So, it's stuck and my official handle is Heat." Heat stared down Edith to let her know the decision was final.

"We were wondering if you heard about the test results from Lugnut's body?" Digger looked at Guardrail as he spoke instead of Heat for some reason.

"Well, not sure why I would know. But thanks for asking." Heat scanned the room for more information.

Guardrail gave in. "The M.P.'s at Lugnut's wake told us you would be our line of communication."

"Well, they didn't tell me, yet. That's for sure."

"Thanks, Heat. Do you know anything about who might have access to this top-secret gas? It may be the key to figuring this whole thing out." Digger locked eyes with the VA policeman this time.

"Well, that is kind of sensitive. But it is well known by everyone here that there is a classified laboratory on the campus here. I shouldn't be telling you, but with the potential for more being hurt, I was told to try and help you any way I could." Heat clearly was uncomfortable about divulging the lab. "But, I'm pretty sure you would learn of it eventually."

Digger grunted like a pig that just unearthed a white, winter truffle. "Oakum's razor." Everyone gawked at Digger. "What?"

Guardrail started laughing. "I'm not sure the stuff used to waterproof old ships is the same as what you meant."

Edith let out a loud hiss. "I have no earthly idea what any of Digger's mumbo jumbo means."

Guardrail continued. "Occum's razor. That is what I think he meant. It means when looking for a solution to a tough problem, the answer with the fewest assumptions is probably right. Even if it is a bizarre answer."

Edith snorted. "I'm still confused."

Dog tried to help her. "Remember the letters from the Grumpy Chicken? We played with them late last night to keep busy after Ginger called us."

Edith tilted her head back. "Oh, yeah. We didn't make heads or tails from it."

Heat jumped in. "I got the razor word. But we couldn't figure out the Oakum part."

Guardrail chuckled. "Neither could we. But Piper, the journalist friend of ours, knew the word and figured it out. And why were you with Edith and Dog late last night?"

"The CO put me in liaison duty. Wanted someone watching them so nothing else happened." Heat turned to Digger. "So, why do you think knowing about the lab is part of this Occam's razor thing."

Digger grinned. "It ain't hard. Top-secret gas, classified lab. Slick and Lugnut spent lots of time at the VA. The gas must have come from the lab."

Heat folded his arms. "We run a tight ship here. I don't know."

Edith threw out. "Even if that were true. It doesn't make sense to me that someone could have gotten into the lab."

Heat nodded in agreement. Then his face went white. "There is one other thing. The more I think about it, it makes more sense. And it explains why the FBI has two agents running around here asking questions."

Edith sat up straight. "Well, spill it. Or your

nickname will be mincemeat when I'm done with you."

Heat smiled at her. "You are a tough one. I like you. But I don't know if I can tell you."

Guardrail assumed his best official voice. "The MP's with the FBI guys standing right next to them told us you would help us and be our line of communication."

Heat put his hands in the pockets of his perfectly pressed blue slacks. "The director of the classified lab has gone missing. He's been gone for a few days and I assumed all the hullabaloo was about that. But you boys have no connection to him or the lab. It doesn't make sense."

Digger snorted. "It doesn't make sense because we haven't found the link. But if there is a link, a lot of what we know fits. The gas from the VA was tainted. The pills from the VA may have been tainted. Now, we learn there is a missing person, someone who runs a classified lab. This all wreaks of a government cover up. We just need to find that last link now."

Dog's voice became squeaky and high. "Me? In a government cover up? They're knocking us off because I used 10W 30 instead of 10W 40 in a general's jeep more than forty years after the fact? I don't think so."

Guardrail smiled. "I've been telling them..."

A pretty nurse came in with some paperwork. "If you sign, here, and here, you can be on your way."

Heat studied her for a moment. "Where's Linzi? I

though she was on today"

"She called in sick." The nurse smiled at Heat and then took the papers back from Dog. "Thanks. Someone will be here in about ten or fifteen minutes to take you out."

Dog moaned. "Dang, can't I just walk."

The nurse laughed. "You been through this more than once, you know the rules."

Dog let out a raspberry. "Not you. You're sweet, I like you. But that rule." He let out another Bronx cheer.

Guardrail laughed at his partner when his phone rang. "Hey, Ginger. Glad you called. Dog is getting out this morning." Digger, Dog, and Edith paid close attention to the call. And Guardrail noticed that Heat did as well. "Wow, the séance told you all that. Well, the pieces are starting to come together. What? Slow down."

Edith glanced at Heat and noticed he looked confused. "You met Star and know she is psychic. Well, sometimes she talks to the other side and asks for their help."

Heat nodded to show he understood. "Yeah, but somehow it's different when it's on TV. Happening in my home town, and with me involved, it's just…kind of creepy."

Edith waved her hand at him. "Oh, don't be silly. You love it. I saw how you looked at Star."

Guardrail hung up and looked at his toes. "You aren't going to believe this. The séance went well. They learned Lugnut was poisoned. And that the killer was a woman. But Ginger also got a call from Ida. Seems a Linzi Howard ordered a bunch of books and stuff on how to be a medium. And she even ordered some stuff through Star's mail order service in Potter's Mill."

Heat took a gulp of air. "Linzi Howard, the nurse that works here?"

Guardrail nodded. "The one and the same."

Digger chuckled. "The grumper is right again. Linzi was close to Slick and Lugnut. Connection made."

Guardrail continued. "It's even a little stranger than that. One of the other things they learned at the séance was that a medium was working with an evil spirit. They think they've been trying to control people's thoughts and actions."

Dog froze. "I have been wondering why I put that stinking gas mask on when I knew it may have hurt Slick. I didn't feel like myself when I did it. Someone could have been controlling me."

Heat cleared his throat. "Is this normal. Have you guys run into this before?"

Edith sternly said, "Not even close. This is fresh ground."

Chapter Nineteen

Slick roared with laughter. "You all comfortable back there?"

Dog had squeezed into the back of Candy's mid-sized sedan with Guardrail and Edith. Guardrail took up almost the whole back seat himself and Edith was perched in his lap. Digger sat in the middle up front, Slick rode shotgun and Candy drove.

"It's good thing I can't move or I would let you know how I really feel." Dog actually had a growl to his voice.

"It's no picnic up here either, I haven't been in the middle seat since I was ten." Digger stared at them through the rear-view mirror.

"It ain't far. And I know the shortest way there. I've known Linzi for years and you will see, she'll be home sick. Just like she called in." Slick's happiness to be out of the hospital could not be contained.

"You were lucky they let us both go this morning. You got more of the gas than I did." Dog needed something to complain about.

"Yeah, but I spent a whole day more than you inside there." Slick was not going to let anything get him down. He was out of the hospital with the love of his life. And his best friend after Lugnut was in town right in the middle of one of his wacky stories. Slick always wanted to part of it, he was a little jealous of Dog's part in the Grumpy Chicken. But now he was part of one of the famous stories.

"That's it over there. Yeah, sweetie, park over here and wait. We're to meet Ginger here before we do anything." Slick pointed to a spot and Candy followed his instructions to the letter.

Once parked they all jumped out to stretch their legs and breath again. Guardrail said, "I knew taking a cab to the hospital was a bad idea." He stretched his back and let out a roar. "That's better. And I told Ginger and Star to bring both cars. We're not piling in like that again."

Slick asked, "Why does she want us to wait?"

"She's afraid Linzi may not be acting alone. If she is the one we are looking for, Ginger wants a plan to stake the place out, surround it with enough people so no one can sneak out." Edith spoke like a general relaying battle plans.

Candy chuckled, "You guys take this stuff pretty serious."

Edith huffed. "You think this isn't dangerous? We're looking for someone who may have murdered one man and just tried to kill your prom date."

Candy pinched her lips and went red. "There's no need to be rude."

Dog chuckled. "It's not being rude at all. Trust me.

She's trying to help you understand the situation. It's hard the first time to comprehend how real and dangerous this all can be."

"You believe in this chicken, for real?" Candy's voice gave away the fact she'd been dying to ask that question.

Guardrail answered. "Yes, we do. I have seen things that made me a believer. And I was more skeptical than you in the beginning."

Edith tittered. "Are you kidding me? The first time ole miss Grumper messed with your pickled eggs, you were madder than a hornet. Then she kept crushing those huge jars of eggs just to mess with you."

Dog laughed. "She's got you there, big guy."

Guardrail scowled at them. "Maybe. But that doesn't change our situation now. This one is weird and I could tell the other reason Ginger wanted us all here is that she's worried about this one. It is different and I can feel it. But what's really weird is I can tell Star, and Ginger, and Piper feel it, too."

Edith pointed up the road to where she was watching. "I think that's Piper coming, and that looks like the rental car we drove here in. They're coming."

Chapter Nineteen

"You all came in that?" Star stared at the mid-sized sedan.

"It was a bit tight." Edith chortled.

I chuckled myself. "That must have looked like those little clown cars the circus used to have when you all got out. I loved when all the clowns came piling out."

"I'm glad you're in a good mood for a stake out. I hate these things." Digger scowled at the house down the road, our target.

Something was telling me not do this, to stop and go back home. But all the pieces fit and we needed to learn what was going on with Linzi Howard. "Alright. You two know your usual job." I stared at Dog and Guardrail.

Dog slumped. "We always watch the back door."

Guardrail added. "Yeah, but that is where the bad guy always tries to escape from. We get to take them down."

Dog murmured. "Somehow, taking down a middle aged nurse was not the first thing I wanted to do once I got out of the hospital."

I continued. "Yes, you two have the back. And Dog, no throwing rocks through the window this time.

Digger you take the west side. And Star and Dixie, you take the east side." That left the north, the front door. "Piper, you're with me. We knock and see if she is home. Edith, you stay here with Slick and Candy, watch for anyone else coming out to the house, like the police or FBI. You call me or Piper immediately if you do."

Edith nodded in reply.

Candy was breathing kind of fast. "Is this really happening. I have never done *anything* like this in my whole life."

Piper studied Candy, then shot a glance to Dixie. "You still think Candy is the killer?"

Dixie laughed, nervously. "Nah, I never really did. I was just joking around with you."

Candy shot glimpses to Slick then to a few of us, trying to figure out why Piper and Dixie were talking about her.

"Stop the chatter. We got work to do. Now let's go. You all need to get into position before me and Piper knock on the front door." I narrowed my eyes and folded my arms. "Git, we need to get this done."

Digger wandered off slowly. "Everybody gets a partner by me. I'm always out on my own."

Piper and I waited at the car for our team to take their positions.

Slick watched, too. "You know how to do this pretty well."

I smiled at him. "We have done this a couple of times now."

It took a minute, but everyone was ready and Piper and I made the walk down the road. We slowly walked up to the front walk and Piper stopped at the base of the path. "Look at that." She was pointing at the mailbox.

I inspected it closely because my brain debated what my eyes saw. There, painted on the side of the mailbox was a likeness of the Grumpy Chicken. Complete with the shackle on its leg. "Seems someone had been reading your articles, Piper."

Piper turned back to make eye contact. "Normally, I would love to meet a fan. But something is telling me that this is not necessarily a good thing."

"I have the same feeling. Star is right. Something is trying to control the situation and is messing with us. Trying to keep us from finding the truth." I stared at the front door. "Well, we're here, it's just a short walk up to the door now. Are we ready?"

"Yep. Let's get to the bottom of this." Piper looked determined and started up the concrete walkway confidently.

I followed and checked to make sure there was nothing unusual in the windows or any sounds that might cause some concern. But it was all quiet and before I knew it, the quaint door knocker was in front of me. So, I used it, gently rapping it a few times. It made an unusual clanking sound, but it was effective because the sound seemed to carry, and it would be hard to miss.

"Maybe you need to hit it a little harder. Here, let me." Piper took the clapper and hammered it five times, like she was trying to drive a nail into wood. "She should have heard that."

We waited, but nothing. Piper took up her sarcastic voice. "If I didn't know better, I might think she isn't home. What do we do now?"

I turned to study the front lawn and each side of the house, checking for our lookouts. They were still there and they shrugged at me, letting me know there was nothing happening.

Then I saw Slick coming up the road in power walk. When he was within earshot he hollered. "She's not home if you used the knocker and she didn't answer. But I know how to get in."

Piper looked at me. "I still say it is all a little too cozy with this VA crowd here in Statesboro."

Slick was up the front walk and out of breath. "Linzi always leaves the downstairs bath window cracked. She is obsessed with letting in fresh air."

Piper shrugged and waved to Dixie and Star. I pointed to the back and waved to Digger. I could tell he understood, because he waved at the two boys in the back to come to the front, then he came to meet us too.

With the gang assembling on the front porch, Candy finally walked up behind everyone. "I'm glad you came over, too. We might have a job for you."

Candy stared at me confused.

Piper laughed. "I was wondering who would have to crawl through that little window. But she is the smallest of us all. How do some woman stay so skinny?"

Candy shook her head no. "I can't break into someone's house. It's wrong."

"Okay. We'll just leave and maybe let the person who hurt Slick get off Scot-free." Guardrail could be persuasive when he wanted to be.

Slick consoled his girlfriend. "I know Linzi well. And she wouldn't mind if we let ourselves in. Heck, she has let herself into Lugnut's place before."

Candy tilted her head back and looked at Slick down her nose. "How do you know that?"

Slick blushed. "I just know. Trust me."

Candy fidgeted with her hands a moment. "Alright. But if we get into trouble, I'm telling the police you made me do it."

About four or five of us replied in unison. "Fine."

Slick went around to the side and boosted Candy up. She was able to lift the window and slide in without trouble. Within thirty seconds the front door opened and we poured into the house.

Slick yelled. "Linzi, you home?"

We all stared at him. I added, "We don't have to tell the whole neighborhood we're here."

"What, I'm just making sure. Now, what are we looking for?" Slick was enjoying this a little too much.

Piper answered. "Anything unusual. You'll know it when you see it."

My attention was on Star walking into the entry. She seemed to be floating on the floor, not really walking on it. I could tell something was guiding her. "Star, are you alright?"

"Yeah. The Grumpy Chicken and Lugnut are trying to work together to help us. But they're being resisted by a presence on their side that I cannot quite make out. It is making it hard." Star stopped and closed her eyes, then held her arms out at shoulders length, and slightly behind her in an odd position. That was when I also realized her hair was flowing in a stream of air that seemed to be blowing in her face. With her arms and hair billowing in a breeze I could not feel or see, it looked like a great wind was blowing the branches on a tree. And then it suddenly stopped.

Star returned to normal and looked at me and smiled.

Candy's voice squeaked from behind me. "What in the world was that all about? It was really creepy and I think I peed a little when her feet came off the floor."

Star could make her voice sound so sweet when the paranormal she lived with everyday scared someone. "I'm sorry. But sometimes things like that happen. And it was a good thing. We need to look for a receipt in the den."

Candy's voice went from squeaky to bull horn in a second flat. "Slick. Git your scrawny bum in here, stat. I need you."

Slick came into the entry sipping a beer. In disgust, I let out a loud exhale. "Where did you get that. And it is only eleven o'clock in the morning."

Candy ripped the beer out of his hands. "Really, you just got out of the hospital, too. Now show Ginger and Star where Linzi keeps her den."

Slick shrugged. "Okay. That is upstairs. Come on." And with that he led the way.

Once inside the den, I shouldn't have been surprised, but I was. A piece of paper glowed in a way that shot a beam of light straight to the ceiling. Slick gasped. "Great Caesar's ghost. If I didn't know better, I would think that's what you're looking for."

Candy was behind him but could see it, too. "You think, Einstein?"

Star calmly walked over and picked up the paper. It stopped glowing as soon as she touched it. She read it then looked up at me. "It's a receipt for a cabin."

Slick went over and took the paper from her and read it. "I know where this is. It's on a river not far here. We can be there in a half hour."

Piper and Dixie made their way upstairs to the scene. Piper confirmed, "I overheard. Looks like we're mobile again. But I don't think we need this whole crew. Some of us should head back to the VA and see if the test results on Lugnut's body are in. And someone needs to tell the FBI what we found here."

I shrugged. "What a glowing piece of paper? All they will see is a rental slip?"

Piper chuckled. "No. I can see you didn't have a chance to look around in here."

So, I did. And I was amazed. The room was packed with books and odd items, one I recognized. It was a crystal ball just like the one Star had in her new age shop. Then I spotted the tarot cards, and the books. There were tons of books on hypnotism and how to be a medium. And I spotted one on how to cast spells. Slowly, I felt a tingle start at the base of my spine and run all the way up. Star had detected a medium might be involved in the séance. And this was too big a coincidence to ignore.

"Holy Merlin. She was serious about this stuff." I couldn't hide my surprise.

Piper chuckled. "Yep, I think this is going to be of interest to more people than just us."

I locked eyes with my journalist friend and sighed. She was right I needed a plan. "Where's Edith?" I just realized she'd been missing the whole time.

Candy answered. "She's knitting in the car. She said she would direct traffic or alert us if anyone tried to interrupt us."

I smiled. "That's our Edith, alright. Slick and Candy, can to go back to the VA with Edith and tell the FBI or VA police what happened at the séance and what we found here. You know about the séance, right?"

Candy nodded, "Yeah, Guardrail told us."

"Okay, tell them what we learned and see if they can share the test results with us. They should confirm poison in Lugnut's body if the spirits were right. And they usually are." I eyed Candy and Slick to make sure they understood. "We'll get directions from Slick to the cabin."

Slick was having too much fun and he thought we were playing a game. It made him a poor candidate to trust with delivering the message to the FBI. But I trusted Edith and I could see in Candy's eyes, she understood how important and dangerous this was.

"Good, you take Slick and Edith in your car to the VA. We'll take the rest of us in Piper's car and the rental. I want the boys with us at the cabin if there's trouble." I spun to confirm the plan with Piper and Star. They nodded, and after Star put the cabin rental receipt in her pocket, we headed out of the den and readied for the next stop on our adventure.

Chapter Twenty

The cabin was beautiful. It sat right on the bank of the river and it was a real log cabin. Even from our distant vantage point, I could see it was made from physical logs and old-fashioned chinking.

Piper must have noticed me checking it out. "It is beautiful and they don't make them like that anymore."

Guardrail shook his head. "Only two girls from Potter's Mill would see the beauty in an old log cabin, and how it's constructed."

Digger grumbled. "Well, no one was home at the last stop. But there is smoke coming from the chimney. Someone's home at this place."

Dixie joined in on the grumbling. "I was fine at the last house, but this is making me a little nervous. I think I can hear banjo music coming from that cabin."

"Remind me why you came with us? What did you think we were going to do?" I looked through the top of my eyebrows at her to make my feelings clear.

Dixie stammered. "I don't know. Meet some interesting people, see some nice places, have some fun. But storming a cabin in the woods inhibited by a wannabe witch is not what I envisioned."

Star gasped. "Witch, that is low. A medium is not a witch!"

Piper laughed. "I thought bartenders were supposed to be good at making friends. But take the two feet of hard counter between her and others out of the equation, and I see it's a different story."

Dixie waved her hand at Piper like she was shooing off a house fly.

Dog pointed. "I think I see some movement in a window. So, I think Digger is right, someone is here. How are we going to do this?"

I picked up a stick and started scratching a square in the dirt with it. Then I drew a long line next to the square. "This is the house, and the line is the river. We can use the river to our advantage. It's big enough and the water is moving fast enough that it would not be easy to cross. So, we need to watch these three sides." I pointed with the stick. "Dog, Guardrail, you take up a position here. Digger, you take up here." I took another look at the cabin, looking for its strengths and weaknesses as if I was trapped inside. "Alright, Star, Dixie, you should be here." I drew an X with the stick for Star and Dixie. "Keep a phone out as we may need to call for help and you should be able to stay out of sight there. Dog, Digger, and Guardrail will have to move quick if something happens, but I think it will work if we take these positions. And that will allow Piper and me to approach and make the knock safely."

I saw everyone study the crude drawing in the dirt and nod. Not a single modification, I was surprised. "Alright, everybody needs take up their positions. Piper and I will wait until you get there and then we'll approach the entrance."

With a surprising stealth, the unlikely team of two motorcycle mechanics, a medium, a bartender, and a gravedigger moved through the woods to prepare for a take down. Piper and I held back a ways to let the others get to their posts.

Once everyone was settled into position, we made for the front door. I never remembered walking so slow to an entrance, and I could tell Piper felt the same way.

When we were about ten feet from the entry, as I was about to ask Piper how we should handle our questions, the large, heavy door swung open with an ominous creak. Linzi took a step out and smiled broadly. "Well, hello ladies. I was wondering when you were going to stop drawing in the dirt and come and say hello."

Piper glanced to me. "She seems to be well informed, wouldn't you say?"

"Maybe, but if you knew we were coming, why did you wait for us?" It was the best I could do on the spot.

"Me and the Bitter Gentlemen have been wanting to spend some private time with you." Linzi smiled and I felt it was how the snake smiled at Eve after he told her to eat the apple.

Piper gagged. "I don't know who the Bitter Gentlemen is, but something stinks to high heaven. You ever clean in there?"

"There was a little experiment I conducted and have

yet to finish. It is getting a little rancid now, but I can tolerate the smell since there is still so much to learn. You want to see?" Linzi's eyes were wild, not like when we met at the wake.

Piper took a peek over to me to see if I would object, but I made no response. She understood and answered for both of us. "We came here to see if we could talk with you a bit more. So, yeah we would love to come in and see what you have done with the place."

Piper led the way and we entered the well-lit interior. In the center of the one room cabin was a man tied to a chair. He was dead, apparently had been there a while since the body was clearly the source of the rancid odor. We slowly walked inside only a couple of steps, staying close to the door. On the dining table, I spotted a pill bottle and started to move towards it.

Piper hissed at me. "What are you doing? Stay here, near the door."

"I need to see something." I went and picked up the little container and then scanned the label. "I see you took an interest in Lugnut's pill bottle like everyone else. But why do I suspect your interest was not in testing the pills?"

"You're right, of course. I took that one from Lugnut's apartment so no one else could test it."

"This little star drawn on the bottle was your mark to find the right bottle, right?"

"They said you were smart, Ginger."

Piper took an annoyed tone, "We get it. You covered up what you did to Lugnut. So, you seem to be comfortable with a dead guy tied to a chair as a centerpiece. Are you going to introduce us?"

"He is no one special. Just someone I needed to get the supplies I needed." Linzi flicked the back of her hand at him like she was sending a plate back to the kitchen of a restaurant.

"I see." Piper took one step back toward the door.

Linzi chuckled. "Don't be so fast to leave. You know who he is why I needed him, don't you?"

I winced. "Maybe. Guardrail mentioned a lab director that was reported missing at the VA hospital."

Linzi hummed a little then said, "Oh, don't be so modest. You know all about the classified lab and you've guessed that I took the gas I needed from there. You know the only way for me to gain access to something like that was to use someone who worked there. And the director was so easy to control. The Bitter Gentlemen showed me how to do it, and it worked perfectly. He even made for a perfect guinea pig to test the blend I made. And as you can see it worked wonderfully. I don't know why it didn't work on Slick though? I think he must have smelled something funny and pulled the mask off too quickly. But Mr. Lab Director here was tied up. So, maybe I miscalculated on that one."

Piper shot back. "But you didn't miscalculate with Lugnut. Your plan worked just fine and induced his heart attack."

"That was easy. I had access to Lugnut's medication and the pharmacy. So, I just had to get the spiked pills back after the deed was done. The old coot had a dozen bottles scattered around the house and I almost did not find the right one. But I did and you can just keep on testing pills from his place now, no one will find anything."

"So, why are you telling us this all now?" Piper cut to the chase. I could tell she wanted out of this cabin.

"I wanted to meet the great Grumpy Chicken gang. The famous gang of misfits who solve murders using some paranormal help. You know, with my wanting to be a famous medium and all."

Star's voice drifted through the open front door. She was moaning.

Linzi's crazy rant continued. "Oh, I didn't tell you. I thought you might come out here to visit. So, I made preparations for potential guests. I can feel her fear and I would guess she senses The Bitter Gentlemen is here."

Dixie appeared in the doorway and was panting heavily and sweating. "Ginger, Star is possessed or something…Oh my God. I will never complain about tending bar again. Just let me survive this and get back to my bar. Is that man dead over there?" Dixie gave a half-hearted point to the dead lab director. "And it smells like low tide at the sewage treatment plant crossed with a skunk's butt in here."

Piper tried to keep her under control. "Dixie, why don't you go back and see if you can help Star. Linzi, you have any advice that might help Dixie?"

Linzi popped like a preteen girl answering her mother. "Nope. Sorry."

Dixie took off so fast I thought I heard that funny cartoon sound someone makes when they move really fast, like a an out of tune slide flute.

Linzi strolled towards us and picked up something off the table. "You see this? It's a trigger. It will start a process of leaking the one triple two gas over there." Linzi pointed at a large tank painted black with a red icon depicting flames. "Once there is enough gas in the room, it will explode and make that big propane tank outside explode, causing an even bigger boom."

Piper shuddered. "Let me guess, we will be inside the cabin when it blows."

"Of course, it just has to be this way. Sorry about that." Then Linzi locked eyes with Piper. "Tell Dixie to bring Star here. And get those three men in the woods to come on in too. I will keep Ginger nice and safe as insurance to make sure you bring them all back."

Chapter Twenty-One

Digger, Dog, and Guardrail were easy to retrieve. They were worried about me since Linzi held me captive while Piper fetched them. They came running to help.

But Dixie and Star were a different story. Star had been afflicted by some sort of spell. Dixie figured out she could get Star to walk towards the cabin, but in no other direction. It was just a matter of holding her hand and leading the way since Star could not see. Her eyes were now deep black pools that seemed to eat light.

Dixie and Star finally showed up and Linzi clapped like a play had just ended. "Oh goody. Now, we all know what is going to happen here, but you can make it easier on yourself if you help me with Star."

Guardrail snarled. "You're nuts. Stop this right now. No one else has to get hurt."

Linzi smiled back at him. "I need you to be quiet. Star and I have some work to do and I cannot be interrupted. Here, make yourself useful. Fetch that rope in the corner over there and tie Ginger and Piper to the chairs." She pointed at the rope.

"Don't do it, Guardrail." Dog's voice revealed fear, but also anger.

Digger added, "Let me do it. I know how to use a rope better than Guardrail."

Linzi eyed the old grave digger and nodded yes. "Alright. And, I can use the big guy to help me with Star."

Linzi took an odd-looking apparatus from a bag and placed electrodes on Stars temples. Then inspected Star's eyes for some reason. "Good, the Bitter Gentlemen has her."

Piper and I were in the process of being tied to the wooded chairs at the table. Piper blurted out, "Who in the blazes is this Bitter Gentlemen?"

Linzi rocked her head like she was deciding something, then she spoke to no one in particular. "Oh well, it can't hurt to tell them." She came over to Piper and checked the ropes. "See, I have always been curious about the paranormal since I could sense things sometimes, and your pub was only about an hour from here so I always imagined taking a trip to check it out. After all the stories Slick and Lugnut told me. But as I read and learned more about being a medium, I stumbled onto a spirit willing to help me speed things up. But he needed help, too. So, we formed an alliance."

Piper asked, "What did you want?"

Linzi shrugged, "To be as good as Star."

"And what did this Bitter Gentlemen want?"

"Revenge. He claims he was wronged by someone very famous and very powerful. But he would not tell me who. He just needed me to do some things on our side to make his revenge happen." Linzi seemed to be getting bored explaining to Piper.

My concern forced me to ask, "Is this going to harm Star? I don't like the look of that contraption."

"Oh, it will kill her. It is the only way. But she's not going to need her skills for much longer, so it would be a shame not to pass them on." Linzi talked like she was annoyed that we did not know what she wanted.

"You can do that? Transfer paranormal abilities?" Piper was stalling, I could tell.

"Well, I think so. I have never actually done it. But the Bitter Gentlemen told me we could."

"Is this the Bitter Gentlemen we are talking to right now?" Piper had her journalist voice and I could tell she was trying to form a plan.

"Sort of. I am his conduit to this side, but it's not possible for him to speak through me."

Digger was scanning the trigger on the table and I saw him look at the big black tank. He asked, "You rigged it to blow, didn't you?"

"Oh, yes dearie. I already told Piper and Ginger all about it. It gets rid of all this evidence, and you and your friends."

Dog whispered to me. "A gas needs to mix with air to explode."

I nodded, "Yeah, she said there would be delay once she triggered it."

Dog added, "I can get the trigger, I think. She has it in the table and I think I'm faster than her."

Linzi stood straight and her voice boomed. "That is not a good idea. And it will only work for me, it has a bio-metric authorization. Now, you seem to be a handful, Dog. I guess I need to handcuff you to the sink." And Linzi proceeded to do just that with Dog protesting all the way. "Now you big guy. I got one more set of cuffs. Let's cuff you to the toilet." Linzi made Guardrail wrap his arms around the small toilet in the tiny bathroom and went back to tending to Star."

Dixie had been silent. I think I even heard her praying at one point. But she chose to speak, "Linzi, where did you get all this stuff?"

She laughed and put her hands on her hips. "You obviously don't know what it's like to work in a veteran's hospital. The VA is full of all kinds of technology and people who know how to use it. And it's so easy to get what you need. These cuffs came from the VA police office. And Mr. lab director here built this trigger for me. He would take his bows, I am sure, if he was breathing."

Linzi looked around the cabin like she was trying to find something. Digger quipped, "Can I help you find something?"

Linzi picked up some more rope. "Nope. Dixie and

Digger, I am sorry but I am plumb out of places to tie or cuff people to. You will have to be tied to each other."

Linzi made them sit on the small bed and tied them together. After checking they were bound tight, she went back to Star seated in the fourth wooden chair that served the lone table in the room. She seemed to fiddle with a few switches on a small black box connected to the electrodes. Then tried again. "Damn it! You said it would work!"

Dog shot back. "Aw, having a bad day are ya?"

"Shut up! I am sooooo angry. And now it appears I have to leave because your friends sent more people out here to help you. All this to leave without Star's powers. Shame, now what am I going to do?"

Piper threw out an idea. "You could let us go."

Linzi went into a rage and grabbed a few of her possessions. Then she grabbed the trigger device and flipped it on. A big red light lit up and gas started to hiss from the big black tank. She let out an evil laugh, then threw the trigger device on the floor. "Sorry to have to run kiddies, but there is no more time for me to work with you." Then she promptly exited.

Digger started grunting and groaning. "Come on, Dixie. Help me. I puffed myself up when she tied us up so it might be loose enough to get out when we had a chance. Well, I think this would be good time to get out of these ropes."

"How could you puff yourself up? You always look puffed up." Dixie stopped talking and starting groaning like Digger. Suddenly the ropes fell off.

"Voila! We only have a few seconds. I am going to drag the tank to the river and throw it in the water." Digger pointed and Dixie understood. They both sprinted to the tank and dragged it to the door. "I can take it from here. No need to put us both in danger." And Digger made off for the river dragging the tank across the ground.

Dixie untied me and Piper and the we tried to get Dog and Guardrail loose. We couldn't find a key but Dixie fashioned a paperclip into a makeshift key and got them both loose. Guardrail stood and rubbed his wrists as he stretched. "That was really uncomfortable. Thanks. Where did you learn to jimmy handcuffs, Dixie."

Dixie smiled at him, "I'll tell you some other time. But right now, we should get out of here."

Dog rocked his head at his cuffs. "Come on, I ain't exactly loving this."

Dixie went over and began jiggling the paperclip key in Dog's cuffs. "Yours are a little…" She never finished the sentence. The explosion was so large it blew out the two small windows of the cabin and removed one of the metal panels from the roof.

Piper was thrown to the floor, but she popped up after a couple of seconds and looked around. She screamed a single word. "Digger!"

Chapter Twenty-Two

One Month Later

Dad and I visited Digger's grave and I brought some flowers. We stood there for a moment and took in the beautiful day. "They gave Digger a perfect spot. It is so beautiful."

Dad nodded. "They sure did, sweetie. He worked this place his whole life, it is fitting he got a nice spot here." Dad took out a little flask and took a sip. The he poured a little on Digger's grave.

"I hate when you do that. It just seems kind of rude to me."

"Ginger, you know better than that. It is an old Irish tradition to give the dead a little taste. It is actually a sign of respect."

"I guess. I'm still overly sensitive to everything I think."

Dad sighed. "It wasn't your fault. No one can figure out how that tank blew. No one."

"I know. But I still feel responsible." I heard the sounds of horses coming and spun to the sound.

Dad didn't move. "You know who it is. He's worried about you."

"It's Sheriff Morrison, yes. But it's Aunt Mae, too."

That made Dad turn and look. He waved at the two as they approached us.

Sheriff Morrison dismounted and came over to the site and shook our hands. He then removed his hat and said a small prayer before speaking. "You've been coming here a lot. Your aunt and I are worried about you. It's been a month and you need to start returning to your life."

"Digger was part of my life. So, it is kind of hard to get back to it."

Aunt Mae came over and put her arm around me. "You knew things could get dangerous. And so did Digger. He once told me, though, that working to solve cases with you made him feel more alive than he thought possible. He loved it, even the weird parts that scared him sometimes. It's what he wanted to do, solve mysteries with you and the gang."

The tears made it hard for me to see. "It is like a nightmare and I keep hoping to wake up and see him all grouchy at the end of the bar."

Sheriff Morrison cleared his throat. "I've heard through the grapevine that Linzi is driving the feds nuts with her spirit talk. I'm just happy they were able to capture her before anyone else was hurt." The Sheriff took an envelope from his pocket. "It would seem Digger made some arrangements and he left you a letter. I brought it for you. Here." He held out an envelope.

Aunt Mae asked, "Are you going to open it?"

"Nope, not now. I'm not ready. But thanks for delivering it." I put the envelop in my coat pocket.

Dad checked the saddles on the horses. "I can't believe you let Mae take her out."

The Sheriff sighed. "To be honest, I can't either."

Aunt Mae hugged me and then climbed back into the saddle. The Sheriff remounted and they rode back to town.

Dad and I took our time and walked back to The Grumpy Chicken. We talked about Mom the whole time.

As we entered the pub, Dog and Guardrail were arguing. Dog insisted, "Why would he want his stool moved. It should stay right here. But we need to put a plague on it."

Dad bellowed, "I'm not putting up with another argument about what to do with Digger's stool. It's commendable that you want to honor your friend, but I can guarantee you he did not want you guys arguing."

Dixie added, "Digger will always be here no matter where his stool is."

Star was sipping a soda and put it down. "I haven't sensed him, yet. But it takes a while for some to get their bearings on the other side. And we all know Digger is not good with directions."

I was happy to see Star back to her normal self. It took

a few days to regain her sensibilities again, but she was now back to being her normal self.

Dog shot back, "He was not good at a lot of things. Like social skills."

Guardrail laughed. "He was different, but he was a good man. I'll never forget when that little house cat took him down."

The laughter just slipped from me. "I forgot about that. Or how he wouldn't let that historian mess with the locket he found."

"Dixie and us were just talking about that a few minutes before you got here." Guardrail glanced to Dixie for confirmation.

"Yeah, we were. And how he never liked the grave digger jokes. But he took it all in stride." Dixie chuckled a little thinking of all the times she gave him a hard time.

Bones bellowed from the back. "You know what I liked about Digger. He never complained about my cooking."

Dixie snorted. "Oh yes he did. We all do, we just don't let you hear to be nice."

The clanking sound told me Bones had dropped his spatula on the grill. And sure enough, he emerged through the swinging door. "My cooking is the best. Why do you have to be so mean?"

Dad yelled at Bones. "Did you drop that dang spatula on the grill again? If you break that grill it's coming out of your paycheck!"

I smiled and was jealous. It seemed my friends were getting back to normal, but it still felt like the grief I carried was crushing and it was even hard for me to breath with effort.

Piper and Ida came waltzing in through the front door. Piper made an announcement. "We got another ten papers to carry the column."

Everyone had resumed life, but not me. I could not get over the loss of Digger. I took the envelope out of my pocket and opened it. It wasn't a long note and it included a ten dollar bill. The note read, "If something happens to me, I know Dog and Guardrail will argue over my stool. But I would like the stool cremated and the ashes spread over my grave. Included with this request is ten dollars to cover a round of beers for Dog and Guardrail, my best drinking buddies, and a small tip for you Ginger. Take care of them, you are strong and smart and we always needed you to lead our motley crew. Your friend always, Digger."

The tears came too fast to control them. I tried to compose myself and turned to Dixie. "Digger just bought a round of beers for Dog and Guardrail, so set them up!"

Dog looked like he was going to be sick. "Is that old coot's ghost here?"

I snickered. "No, he left a note that I just got today. Here you can read it. It tells us what to do with his stool."

Guardrail came over and took the note from me. After reading the message he laughed and addressed his business partner. "You aren't going to believe this, he wants us to burn the stool and sprinkle the ashes on his grave."

Dog raised his eyebrows. "What? Well that's a new one. But if that is what he wants, okay!"

Star jumped like she got a little electric shock, then she locked eyes with me. "The Grumpy Chicken helped Digger, and he knows you are all mourning him. But he doesn't want that. And he feels guilty about burning the stool, but he just can't have someone else taking it."

Dixie hooted. "Now there's a vision. Digger and the Grumpy Chicken. Which one you think is the scariest now? My money is on Digger. He was way grumpier than the chicken."

Dog and Guardrail laughed. "I think you're right, Dixie. The old grumper has her hands full now with Digger. But there is only one thing for us to do." Guardrail raised his glass. "To Digger."

Everyone in the pub raised their drinks, too. And they repeated, "To Digger!"

Thanks for Reading

I hope you enjoyed the book and it would mean so much to me if you could leave a review. Reviews help authors gain more exposure and keep us writing your favorite stories.

You can find all of my books by visiting my Author Page.

Sign up for Constance Barker's New Releases Newsletter where you can find out when my next book is coming out and for special discounted pricing.

I never share or sell your email.

Visit me on Facebook and give me feedback on the characters and their stories.

Catalog of Books

The Witch Sisters of Stillwater

Hoodoo and Just Desserts

A Shade of Murder

That Ol' Black Magic

A Whole Lotta Witchin Goin On

The Sinister Case Series

The Sinister Secrets of the Snake Mirror

The Sinister Secrets of the Deadly Summoner

The Sinister Secrets of the Enchanting Blaze

The Grumpy Chicken Irish Pub Series

A Frosty Mug of Murder

Treachery on Tap

A Highball and a Low Blow

Cursed With a Twist

The Chronicles of Agnes Astor Smith

The Peculiar Case of Agnes Astor Smith

The Peculiar Case of the Red Tide

The Peculiar Case of the Lost Colony

Murder or Bust

Pinched, Pilfered and a Pitchfork

A Hot Spot of Murder

Witchy Women of Coven Grove Series

The Witching on the Wall

A Witching Well of Magic

Witching the Night Away

Witching There's Another Way

Witching Your Life Away

Witching You Wouldn't Go

Witching for a Miracle

Teasen & Pleasen Hair Salon Series

A Hair Raising Blowout

Wash, Rinse, Die

Holiday Hooligans

A Caffeinated Crunch

A Frothy Fiasco

Punked by the Pumpkin

Peppermint Pandemonium

Expresso Messo

A Cuppa Cruise Conundrum

The Brewing Bride

Whispering Pines Mystery Series

A Sinister Slice of Murder

Sanctum of Shadows

Curse of the Bloodstone Arrow

Fright Night at the Haunted Inn

Mad River Mystery Series

A Wicked Whack

A Prickly Predicament

A Malevolent Menace

The Monkey's Eyebrow Tea Room Series

A Tiny Bite of Murder

Murder on the Ghost Walk